LET ME JUST SAY THIS

Dedication

For anyone who has a dream. It might be deferred for a while, but as long as it is your dream, make sure you pursue it. Make it happen or forever wonder what if.

Acknowledgments

I would like to thank HIM from whom all blessings flow.

I would like to thank all of my friends. Because of you, this is a dream turned into a reality.

I would like to thank my kids, Kiera, Zac Jr., Greg, Justin, and RaShaunda. I couldn't ask for better young adults.

I would like to also thank LZ and Zavier, Jayden, Tyson, and now the diva, Khloe and baby Isaiah; Nina loves you more and more each day.

To Renesha, always good for a laugh or two.

To my Mattawoman family, I love you to death. Thanks for the push to get me moving and the "mini- meetings" in the conference room.

Shelia, you are like my mother and always there for a good laugh, dirty joke and a good cursing out when necessary.

To Cliff, thanks for all of the laughter in the "morning lounge".

To Shirley, I love you girl. To my sister; although far in distance, still close to heart.

To my brother Mike, well, what is there to say? To my other children, Nu-Nu and Rico and Kelly I love you very much. To Yvonne Medley, thank you for sharing your writing group with me and encouraging me and congratulations on your new novel.

Ok people, Let me just say this: This is the work of an overly active imagination. Don't call the police, and don't overthink it. Just enjoy it and happy reading.

Chapter 1

He shook his hand while trying to stop the sting, "See what you make me do? Why you always have to pluck my fucking nerves? Why can't you leave shit alone when I say so? You make me so fucking mad I can't see straight! Shit!"

Kevin left the room.

He makes me sick, Cheryl thought as she walked into the bathroom to wash her face and calm down. I'm so sick of this. As she turned toward the mirror, she shook her head.

"When are you going to leave him? He slaps you around whenever he gets the inkling to, and it's not even like he cares about your feelings," she said out loud.

As she started to giggle, she felt as if she was losing her mind.

Kevin went to the den and poured himself a drink.

"Shit! Ungrateful! That's what she is." It wasn't like she could hear him screaming to himself. "Why can't you just take no for an answer? Always nagging me! I said no the first four times you asked, yet you had to keep pushing me!"

He took a gulp from the glass and sat it on the table and walked quickly back upstairs.

"Look, maybe you can go with me sometime, but stop acting like some spoiled brat that can't get her way. If and when I want you to go with me, I'll take you. You understand?"

He was speaking to her as if he were speaking to a three year old.

"Who are you talking to?" she shouted.

"Who do you think I'm talking to?"

"Let's see, it's you and me in here. Now who do you think I'm talking to?"

Cheryl brushed by him and he grabbed her arm. Cheryl pulled away from him. He spun her around and before she could say another word, he slapped her so hard she bit the inside of her mouth.

Kevin shoved her against the wall, and as she tried pushing him away, he slapped her so hard she saw blackness for a split second. As he started walking away, Cheryl mumbled.

"What the fuck did you say?"

"Nothing," she whispered

"Don't try and whisper now, if you got shit to say, say it out loud!"

"All I said was, why you always gotta be pushing and hitting on me?"

"Don't you ever fucking question me," he said, slamming her against the wall, over and over again. As she tried to walk away, he pushed her once more, this time sending her to her knees.

Chapter 2

How could he be so cold? How had their marriage gotten to this point?

She was only 40 years old, but felt like a woman of 60. Her body had grown as tired as her mind had. They had been married for 17 years, but it felt more like a lifetime. Donnell and Kayla were wonderful children, never mind that Kevin thought Donnell was more feminine than Kayla. They lived in an exclusive gated community in Southern Maryland and she had everything a woman could want, except for the one thing every woman wanted: the love of a man.

"Yeah, book three tickets to Atlanta," Kevin said into the phone. "I'll let Rebecca know that she will also go with us." After a slight pause, he continued. "If you want her to go, you have to spring for her ticket. Why do you think Cheryl isn't going? I am trying to enjoy myself and take care of business and being nagged is not a part of the plans." He laughed out loud. "Nigga, you are crazy. Holla."

Cheryl walked in just as he finished his conversation.

"Why can't I go with you this time?" she inquired. "You always say, next time, next time, but that doesn't happen." She followed him from the den and up the stairs to their bedroom.

"Look, I won't have this conversation with you again. I don't have time to baby-sit."

"Baby-sit! I ain't no fucking baby. I am your wife and all I am asking is that I go with you this time. Is that too much to ask?"

"Look, every damn time I get ready to go outta town, I gotta hear this from you. You are not going and that's the end of the fucking conversation!"

Kevin stormed out of their bedroom and slammed the door behind him.

Chapter 3

Ten years earlier

Cheryl had planned every detail of Kevin's coming out party for K & B Alliance. She had ordered the best wine, had the best caterer money could afford, and even hired a wait staff. She had gotten her hair done and even got a manicure and pedicure. She had driven all the way to Neiman Marcus on Wisconsin Avenue in D.C. to find the perfect blue dress. Blue was her favorite color and always made her feel better.

After putting her dress on, she looked herself over in the full-length mirror and smiled. She felt sexy. Kevin had on a black Madison pinstriped suit by Brooks Brothers, which she had had tailored to fit his athletic build. He had on a midnight blue shirt with black tie and pocket square. He smelled of musk and shea butter. He had gotten his hair cut two days earlier, because he didn't like to have his hair cut on the day of an event. His goatee was neatly trimmed, just like she liked it, and he had bought himself a new Dallas star earring for his left ear. It seemed as if his light brown eyes had somehow gotten lighter overnight. To say he was as vain as any woman was an understatement. Kevin looked so good, if the guests weren't starting to arrive, she would have jumped his bones.

They opened the door to their first guests and hugged Calvin and his wife Ann.

"How are you guys doing, so great you could make it." Kevin said as he gave Ann a polite hug and kiss.

"Wouldn't miss this for anything in the world." Calvin said as he gave Kevin a hearty handshake and reached for Cheryl's hand and gave it a kiss.

Ann pulled Cheryl to the side and told her how much she liked her new dress and Cheryl gave compliments to Ann as well.

"Kevin so tell Ann how you managed to get this company off of the ground and keep your wife happy. Doing the same thing is proving to be a lot harder than either of us could think of." Calvin said as they walked from the door and further into the party.

"Let's just say that you have to have an understanding and when you both understand that it is going to be better to be your own boss than to work for someone else, than the sacrifice becomes worth it."

"I totally agree." Cheryl chimed in as she looked lovingly at her husband.

"Man, this is over the top. Your wife is an excellent hostess. I am going to have to have Mary call her when we get ready for our next party. She pulled out all the stops," Malik said to Kevin, shaking his hand.

Kevin heard laughter coming from the other side of the room and went to see what the crew was up to. The old crew consisted of men ranging in age from 50 to 60. They had helped to finance Kevin and Black's business. As he walked up he could hear the conversation.

"Man, you see that dress? Ooo Weee, I wish I was the material because I would be rubbing up on that all night long," James said.

"Nigga, you crazy! But you ain't never lied. You see those shoes? What I wouldn't do to have them legs wrapped around me all night," Joe commented. As Kevin approached, they all gave each other looks.

"Man, great party, and better scenery. You know what I mean?" James said, while slapping Kevin on the back. Kevin knew there were some fine honeys here, because he told Cheryl to make sure and invite some of her college friends. One that he wished she had omitted was her friend Dee. That girl was too ghetto for his taste.

"Yeah, most of them are single, but y'all better slow your old asses down. I am not going to be calling 911 tonight because y'all can't act your age."

"Look young blood, if 911 is going to be called, we would be the one calling them. These girls wouldn't be able to handle this," Joe said as he grabbed his crotch. They started laughing.

As Kevin walked off he overheard Derek say, "Y'all can have those women. If he wasn't my boy, I would be scooping her right from under him."

"Still got it bad, huh?" Joe asked.

"Why y'all gotta be so damn loud; but man, what I wouldn't do to have those shoes in the air all night long." The group started laughing again, unaware that Kevin was still listening. Kevin went upstairs and saw Cheryl bending over, changing her shoes.

"What in the hell are you doing up here? The party is downstairs."

"I'll be down in a minute, just slipping into some more comfortable shoes."

"Put the other ones back on," he said through tight lips.

"Kevin, it's fine. I bought these to match the dress and no one will know any different."

"I will."

"Look, let's just go downstairs and enjoy the rest of the party. I'll put them back on later." She said with a sly smile and a wink. She moved up to him to let him know how aroused she was by him. He sidestepped her, picked up her shoes and threw them in her direction.

"Put the fucking shoes back on."

"Lower your voice before our guests hear you. What is your problem? My feet are killing me. Besides, the party is in full swing and I doubt anyone will even notice."

"I will notice," he said, catching her by the arm. "You should have thought about that before you bought them. Now put the damn shoes back on. I am not going to tell you again."

"Get your damn hands off of me! Who in the hell do you think you are!?" Before another second slipped by, he had slapped her so hard she swallowed the mint she had been sucking on.

"It can't be that serious," she said after she stopped coughing.

"Oh, but it is," he said.

He watched her as she hooked the strap on her shoe, got up and started for the door. He gave her a push. He saw the tear slide from her eye but he wasn't going to let her ruin this night for him.

Chapter 4

Cheryl walked back downstairs to the party in full swing. The guests were laughing and the food was being served just as she had planned. The wait staff was doing a great job making sure that no guest had to ask for a drink or food.

"Girl, you out did yourself. I know Kevin is thrilled," Dee said.

"Well, you know I try, but it never seems to be enough" she whispered.

"What did you say?"

"Nothing."

What's up? Why is your mouth tight? What did he do?"

"Nothing, he didn't do anything."

"Why you gonna lie to your girl? You know I see right through that face,"

"Girl, nothing. I'm just tired and my feet are aching, plus I'm ready for bed."

"Oh, I bet you are…I'm jealous. He is looking mighty tasty. Matter of fact, he is looking good enough to eat," Dee said, winking.

"Get your damn mind out of the gutter. Besides he looks all right."

"Hello? We must not be looking at the same man. Girl, your husband is too fine tonight, and I see the way that Rebecca woman is watching him. Like he is a T-bone and she got the steak sauce. Sluurrrrp." Cheryl laughed a little too loud, which caught the ear of Kevin.

He walked over to them and announced, "I need you to meet some of my clients." As he pulled Cheryl in one direction, Dee headed in the opposite.

"Don't be so damn ghetto. Goddamn, every time you get around her you forget yourself."

"I was only laughing at…"

Kevin grabbed her upper arm and pulled her along with him, "Mr. Townsend, I want you to meet my wife, Cheryl."

Mr. Townsend extended his hand to hers and kissed it. Who does that?

"Nice to meet you. I must compliment you on such a great party. Kevin, you have a beautiful wife, if I may say so. You are one lucky man," he said, while slapping Kevin on the back.

"Bet you can't wait to get her alone," he added.

Cheryl tried to excuse herself but Kevin grabbed her and kissed her so passionately that she nearly came right there. As she walked away, or maybe floated away would be a better phrase, her feet didn't hurt anymore.

"Don't hurt her," she heard Mr. Townsend say behind her as she walked to the bar.

James walked over to them and commented, "Just make sure you don't hurt yourself either. I know you going to have those legs high tonight."

They all shared a laugh. Men will be men and Kevin had to put up with them because they were his backers, but Cheryl felt she had to tell Kevin that she didn't appreciate the comments. Whenever those men were together, and liquor was involved, they were vulgar and disgusting and they felt that just because they gave Kevin money that gave them the right to make those disgusting comments.

At two a.m. the party finally came to an end and after the last of the staff had cleaned and gotten paid, Cheryl was happy to head upstairs. She had a blister on the back of a heel. As she took off her dress she let it hit the floor and headed towards the shower. She needed the hot water to relax her muscles before trying to get some sleep. As she stepped out of the shower and came into the bedroom, Kevin met her with a backhand.

"What in the hell..." she said as she stumbled backwards

"Bitch, if you ever dress like that again, I'll take your fucking head off!"

"What are you talking about? I thought you liked my..."

"What, you actually thought I liked you walking around here like some whore!"

"Why didn't you say anything?" she asked while rubbing her face.

"The party was starting and you waited just long enough so that I couldn't say anything," he screamed.

"Damn, it is not that serious," she said as she turned back toward the bathroom.

"What did you say to me?"

"I said it is not that serious."

He grabbed her by the hair, and swung her around. "Oh, but it is that serious!" Out of the corner of her eye she saw the scissors and realized that her dressed was destroyed.

"Why did you do that? You are crazy." she shouted.

"Yes I am. You got that right, I am crazy!

"You think I want to hear how my business partners want to fuck you? You ain't nothing but a tramp and I will show you!" He started unzipping his pants and she brought her leg up between his, hard. As he rolled off of her, she scrambled to the bathroom, but before shutting the door, he was in on her again. This time he punched her so hard, she instantly saw stars. He started dragging her out of the bathroom by her hair.

"I'll show you!" He pushed her to the floor and jumped on top of her

"Stop, Kevin!"

"You think I want to hear what some fucking old men want to do to my wife? Do you?" She shook her head from side to side; causing his hand to slip away from her mouth.

"Kevin, please stop! I'm sorry." she was screaming

11

hysterically by now.

"You better not let me hear no shit like that ever again. You hear me?" Kevin said as he jerked her up from the floor. "Get your fucking ass up!" he swung her around

"Kevin! I'm sorry! I'm sorry!" She was pleading now. "Kevin please!"

"Shut the fuck up! I'm going to treat you just like the whore that you were tonight." He bent her over the chair and entered her roughly.

"Please you're hurting me! Please!" she screamed.

He was in a frenzy at this point. His eyes were bulging and sweat dripped down his face like a man possessed. He had her in a choke hold and she tried to gain leverage so that he couldn't squeeze the life from her.

"Don't you ever walk around here like that again, do you hear me!" The physical pain had long stopped but as he finished, she knew the hurt would be there for a while. He shoved her down as if he was disgusted by the sight of her. She pulled herself up and dragged her sore body to the bathroom. She turned on the shower, stepped in and let the water soothe her. She let the water fall down her body and as it did, her tears did too. She climbed out and fell to the floor as the room began to spin. He slammed open the bathroom door, looked down at her on the floor and rolled his eyes.

"I'm sorry." she whispered. "It won't happen again."

"It better not," he said and continued past her into the shower.

Chapter 5

Cheryl woke up and felt much better. Her headache was gone, and so was Kevin. Kevin had left her a note saying he was having his car detailed and to give the kids some money for dinner because when he got back he was going to take her out to dinner. Yeah, that cycle was starting again. Which part of this was it again? Oh yeah, it was the "I'm sorry and it won't happen again" part. She walked into the living room and saw Donnell sitting there watching television. She touched his shoulder and when he turned around, she pushed the money into his hand.

"Oh, taking you to dinner?" Donnell said.

"Watch your mouth,"

"Whatever,"

"Look, no matter what he does or does not do, he is your father and you have to respect him."

"Wrong. He doesn't want to act like a father to me. He only has one child and that would be his precious Kayla. I'm sure he can't wait until I leave this dump."

"Donnell, why would you say something like that? You know he loves you too."

"Does he? Because I can't tell." Mom, why do you always do that?"

"Do what?" she asked as she stopped and turned back towards him.

"Take up for him. I mean, he beats you down and then he throws you a bone, and then you act like nothing has

13

happened." It's embarrassing!" he brushed by her and started for the stairs

"Donnell," she called after him but he kept walking. She walked up behind him as he reached his room and he slammed the door in her face. She placed her hand on the door and spoke in a faint voice. "I'm sorry if you are upset with me and your dad, but I am trying to make things better. I know you will be out of here as soon as you graduate and I can't blame you. I just hope you understand that things are not as easy as just walking out. I have you and Kayla to think about. That's all I worry about. I would never let him hurt you."

Donnell swept his door open and walked back towards his window. "But you do. Every time he puts his hands on you, it hurts us. Kayla doesn't even hear it anymore. She learned to tune you out. Mom, my room is closer, I can hear you. All the time I hear you. I hear you crying when he is calling you names and I hear you when he is doing worse to you."

Silent tears fell from her eyes, "I'm sorry sweetie." she went over to him and gathered him in her arms and they swayed back and forth.

Donnell spoke in a soft tone, "You know I know he calls me gay all the time,"

"But…" she started to say

"Don't worry about it mom. I don't care."

"Maybe if you bring some…"

"Seriously mom, do you honestly believe I would bring anyone over here? Hell I don't know what I'm going to walk in on half the time. I'll continue to do what I have always done, hang out with my friends at their house."

She kissed him on the cheek and walked off. She knew her baby wasn't gay, and even if he were; he was still her baby. His father never took the time to even sit down and talk to Donnell because, in his words, "He's just a little too meticulous about his clothing and hair." Hell, he got it honest. Kevin did the same thing but when you pointed that out to him, well now; that was just crazy talk. God forbid anyone think he was gay. If and when Donnell decided that he would bring someone home, she just hoped it would be before whomever got pregnant.

She continued to her bedroom and called Dee. After three rings, Dee finally picked up.

"Hey hussy, what's shaking?"

"Nuttin but my ass," Dee replied

"No really, what are you doing?"

"Nothing, chilling. Waiting for my man to come on over and scratch my itch."

"Oh, back to men this week?"

"Bitch, please. Ain't nothing like a good sized man."

"Unless....?"

"It's a good licking woman."

"Eww, you are so damn nasty!" Cheryl laughed.

"Girl, please, don't get all stuck up. I forgot. You don't know what you are missing. Besides that fine ass man of yours scratches and licks whatever you want."

"Girl, please. First of all, I ain't missing nothing and secondly, he ain't licking or scratching nothing here but his own itchy ass."

"What! Are you telling me that Kevin ain't licking your lollipop? Please if that were my man, that nigga wouldn't get up until he had eaten all what was on his damn plate."

"Tsk, please. If he wanted to, I wouldn't let him."

"You crazy as hell!"

"Please, believe me when I tell you, I ain't interested in his mouth being nowhere near that. Hell, especially since I don't know where his damn mouth has been."

"Girl, you ought to quit."

"I'm serious, that nigga is probably eating somewhere else, so let him have it. I'd probably not like it anyway."

"All the reason you need to make him eat until he gets tired"

"Please, he'd probably eat so fast he'd give himself indigestion, and then get mad if I said I was still hungry."

"So?" Dee said.

"What do you mean, so? I'd rather not deal with the hassle" Cheryl said as she stretched out on her queen-sized bed and drew the burgundy and gold pillow under her head.

"You are crazier than shit. Ain't no way that nigga would be selfish and not let me get mine.

"Well, that's you."

"You are crazy. If I don't get mine, I am letting a nigga know."

"And what good does that do?"

"That puts a nigga on notice, that he better finish the job or I will call somebody that can."

"You will not," she laughed.

"Who, you must be tripping. I know I put it on him and he better damn straight put it on me or I'm gonna have to talk about his ass or get Karletta to finish the job."

"You are a mess," Cheryl said, laughing.

"You damn right, but a satisfied one. Now what the hell did you want?"

"Nothing really, I just wanted to talk to your crazy ass."

Dee commented on how crazy Cheryl was for not having her toes curled and instantly Cheryl was in a bad mood.

"I gotta go."

"Girl, get a damn grip. Now you wanna get off the phone. Look is Kevin going out of town soon?" she asked.

"Yeah, why would you ask?"

"Just taking a stab in the dark because you always get like this when he does. So how long will he be gone this time?"

"Four days I think, Thursday through Sunday." She said as she pulled the phone away from her ear to see who was calling. She hit the ignore button and continued listening to Dee.

"Oh, oh. Party time."

"Naw, not for me, I won't have a babysitter for the kids."

Cheryl said.

"Girl, no you didn't just play the kid card. Donnell is what, 16, 17 years old and little Miss Kayla is 12 years old. They aren't babies anymore. I am sure they can be without mommy for a couple of hours. We are gonna live it up this weekend."

"I don't want to leave them..."Cheryl continued.

"Snap out of it. We are gonna have some nice clean fun." Dee said as she pulled the door open and saw her date standing there decked out in all black with his diamond stud sparkling like the sun off the ocean. She smiled and winked as she stepped aside.

"If it involves you, it can't be considered clean." Cheryl said.

"Ha Ha. Don't get slapped hussy." Dee said as she slid herself behind him and ran her free hand over his smooth bald head.

"Yeah Yeah."

"Don't make me hang up this phone." Dee said with fake attitude.

"You wouldn't hang up on me."

"You wanna bet? My ride just got here and I need to board that train." she said as he turned around and pressed himself against her naked body and began nibbling at her neck. "ooohhh."

"Get a room," Cheryl said as she heard the tone in Dee's voice change.

"Ok." She said as she moved her head to the side to give him a little more access to her spot.

"Really? Cause I still hear you." Cheryl laughed. She heard the dial tone.

Cheryl hugged the pillow a little tighter and smiled to herself. She didn't know what she would do without her best friend. After the last few minutes, she suddenly felt tired, so she turned over on her side and decided to get a few minutes of sleep before dinner.

Chapter 6

"Hey sleepy head. Go get dressed," Kevin said as he nudged her awake.

"I really don't feel like going anywhere tonight." Cheryl answered as she turned over.

"Aw, come on. We will have fun." He said to her back.

"That's ok. Besides, I have a headache anyway."

"See that's a good reason to get out of the house. You are always saying I don't take you anywhere, and then see what happens when I try. You don't want to go," Kevin said while standing upright, "I'm not going to beg your ass." He said as he walked towards the bathroom.

"Ok, dang, I will go." She said as she turned over and caught a glimpse of him before he shut the door.

"Well, don't be so damn happy about it." He said from behind the door. He came out of the bathroom and saw her standing at her closet and wished he could withdraw the invite but he had already made a big deal out of it, so he went to his office while he waited for her to be ready.

Kevin was in his office talking to Black.

"She acts like this is the end of the world," he said into the phone. "That would be cool if it were true. Every time I go out of town she acts this way. You would think she would know by now to just stop asking me. Anyway, I didn't call you to talk about this. I'm calling your late ass, so you know to be on time at the airport." his laughter filled the room like an echo in the Grand Canyon.

"Whateva, Nigga, you always the last one to board. Don't get left. This meeting is too important for you not to be there. When this deal happens, K & B Alliance will be on the map. Look I'll talk to you later. I'm going to take her out so I can keep her damn mouth closed until I get back." Kevin hung up the phone and took a swig from his glass and leaned back in his leather chair and closed his eyes. He had worked on building up this company and now it was paying off.

Chapter 7

"Cheryl! Damn, you ain't ready yet?" Kevin yelled in the bathroom.

"Do I look ready?" she asked low enough that it wouldn't cause her a problem.

"No…but you do look mighty sexy standing there." he said as he walked behind her and kissed her neck.

"Baby, you feel so good," he said as his hands untied her robe and found her breasts. "Turn around," he whispered. His hands ran down her body and back up to her small breasts.

"Oh Cheryl." he groaned. "You know what I want." he said as he put his hands on her shoulders and guided her to her knees.

"Oh damn, girl. Don't go so quick."

He pulled her up to him and kissed her roughly and fell to his knees. He began kissing her thighs and licking up to her opening. He could feel the heat from her and slid his tongue further up, brushing against her fine hair. He heard her gasp from above him and he let his hands slide down her round ass and back up to where his tongue left a wet trail upwards.

"Baby, I need to be inside of you," he moaned. Standing, he pressed himself into her, his hips pumping and grinding fast.

"Oh, baby. Give it to me," he said as he grabbed a handful of hair and yanked her head back.

His rhythm picked up and he felt her begin to respond to his body. She began meeting his every stroke.

"Oh, baby. Yes, just like that." His hands fell from her hair and tightened around her waist as he pulled her hips into his. He slammed his body into her. After he released he continued grinding into her. He slipped out of her and kissed her neck.

"Let me go and get cleaned up and get dressed," she said as she stepped away from him.

"Damn, that was good. Sometimes you can be sexy, when you want to be."

She continued towards the bathroom and turned the water on and stepped into the shower. Kevin walked in behind her.

"Goddamn, it's hot in here, why you insist on having the water that hot. I am surprised you haven't burned yourself yet. Shit, I can't shave in here with the mirrors all fogged up. You are so damn selfish. You knew I needed to shave. Shit! I'll be in the guest bathroom."

He slammed the door behind him and then opened it back, "Don't be too damn long. I have already wasted enough time," he said as he closed the door again.

She felt like she could have her marriage back and have her husband back. She just needed to be a bit more patient and it would work out. She climbed into the shower with a new outlook on her life.

Chapter 8

Senior Year

Cheryl only heard part of Mr. Angelo's question.

"Umm, I'm sorry. I didn't hear you."

"Cheryl, do you feel alright, you don't look so good."

"No, can I please go to the nurse?" He wrote her out a pass and she left class. She walked into the nurse's office, knowing full well her dad would never leave work to pick her up.

"Mrs. Dickens, can I lay down for a little while? I don't feel well."

"Let's check your temperature first."

"I know I don't have a fever, my stomach just hurts."

"Ok, but by the next period you will have to go to class."

Cheryl stretched out and all she could hear was Shaun's accusing tone. The bell sounded way too soon, so she got her books and headed to her next class.

"Cheryl, Wait up girl." Cheryl never broke stride.

"Where you been, I went to your last class and someone told me you were sick or something." Dee said as she finally caught up to her.

"Just needed to lay down for a minute, that's all."

"Why you let dat ho get you all upset? I would have just kicked her ass and been done with it."

"It ain't even worth it," she replied.

"Just don't let her get to you. Ignore her." Dee said just as Shaun walked by and grabbed her hand.

"Don't," she snapped at him and snatched her hand

away. She walked off in a fog.

All afternoon, Cheryl heard people whispering about how Brenda was gonna get her. She walked to her bus alone, wishing that Shaun was there. She waited before getting on, hoping to see Shaun to apologize, but he never came. She rode home near tears the entire ride. She couldn't get off the bus soon enough, walking to her house with tears streaming down her face and went straight to bed.

"Cheryl. Cheryl." She glanced at her clock and it read 5:30 pm.

"Ugh." She tried to clear her head but it felt like she had marshmallows for brains.

"Cheryl. Telephone."

She was finally able to comprehend that she wasn't dreaming. "Who is it?"

"Shaun."

"Can you take a message? I'm sleeping," She said as she laid her head back on the pillow.

"If you were sleeping you wouldn't be talking to me, now get up and get this phone." her mom yelled again.

She stomped into the kitchen and yanked the phone up off of the table.

"What." She grumbled into the phone.

"Hey, boo."

"Oh, so now I'm your boo? Could have sworn I was a stranger, since you never walked me to my bus or I didn't' see you anymore during the day."

"I didn't say that." Shaun said with a little attitude.

"Sure you did," she said with much more anger.

"Look, I'm sorry. I was wondering…"

She cut him off, "I gotta go."

She hung up the phone and felt like she had lost her best friend. She didn't know what a broken heart felt like but she was sure this was it. Her head started to hurt again, she went back to lie down and felt miserable. For the next week, she flunked two tests, barely spoke to Dee and didn't acknowledge Shaun. She was in her own personal hell, and to top it off, her mom and dad were leaving for the weekend. They gave her and her sister, Angel, the usual speech. No company, no going out and no talking on the phone after 11PM. That meant just the opposite to her sister. Before the driveway could get wet from the falling rain, Dewayne pulled up in his brown hooptie. Angel let him in and they headed to the basement to watch television. The phone rang just as she was heading back to her room.

"Cheryl, wait, don't hang up. Just listen. I'm sorry. You know me better than that. It's just that a lot of stuff is going on and I got a lot on my mind."

"I thought I did, but I'm not so sure anymore."

"Come on C, you know me...c'mon babe" Shaun said with a laugh "Baby, I'm really sorry. I promise it won't happen again. I miss you babe."

"I miss you too," she replied, and at that moment, she knew what she needed to do. "Shaun, you want to come over?"

"For how long?"

"Until tomorrow."

"Yeah, right. Now you know your mom would never go for that."

"They ain't home. They will be gone all weekend."

"Word?"

"Word."

"I'll be there in an hour," he said and hung up.

She hung up and had a huge smile on her face. Tonight was the night. Well at least she thought it would be.

But now that she had a chance to think, maybe that wasn't such a good idea. She was in no hurry to give up the goods; hell, they had been dating two years and he ain't never pressured her about it.

She heard the basement door open and Angel and Dewayne came upstairs.

"You want something to eat?" her sister asked her.

"Naw."

"Why don't you tell Shaun to come over?"

"Already did."

"Ooo, it's about time."

"Get your mind out of the gutter."

Angel rolled her eyes, "What, I'm just saying, bout time you give that boy some."

"Ain't nobody say he was getting any."

"Well, you better, because if you don't then somebody will," Angel said as she threw her hand up and pushed past Cheryl.

"Whatever. We have something more than him just wanting to sex me up."

Angel sucked her teeth and headed out the door.

Chapter 9

There stood Shaun. He was all sweaty and had blood on his shirt. When she looked at his face, there was a golf ball where his eye should have been.

"Oh my god," she yelled while pulling him inside the door. She led him to the kitchen and pulled out the chair for him and grabbed the kitchen towel from the counter and snatched open the freezer. She put a handful of ice in it and handed it to Shaun. Before she could ask a question, Shaun was already talking.

"That Nigga ain't my father. He is dead to me. He ain't had no right putting his hands on my moms again. I bet he wished he hadn't."

She stroked his hand as she kneeled in front of him, "What do you mean, he wish he hadn't?"

"I kicked his ass. I treated him like a pickpocket who stole my wallet. I told him before to keep his hands off of my moms and he must have thought I was kidding. I tried to put my hand down his throat."

"Is your mom ok? What did he hit her for? Why didn't you just call the police? What did your grandma do?"

"If you shut the fuck up for a minute, I'll tell you," he yelled as she pushed him away and stood up and walked to the sink to wring out the towel.

He continued talking. "After we hung up, I jumped in the

shower and could hear them arguing again. She was telling him she was sick of hearing how he was screwing everything in the building and he was saying some crap about how he is tired of her bitching about stupid shit. My moms told him she wanted him to leave and he told her some shit about paying all the bills and he wasn't going anywhere. Like he has a damn job. He ain't work nowhere for as long as I can remember. My mom told him he could roll out and that she was tired of all of his bullshit and him being lazy and he went the hell off. He started throwing crap around the apartment and she yelled at him to get out or she would call the cops and he went after her. I heard him hit her and heard her tell him to let her go, so I jumped out of the shower and threw on some pants. By the time I ran into their room, he was beating her like a man. She had blood everywhere on her face and all I knew was he wouldn't hit her again. I yelled at him to get off of her and he turned and told me to leave if I didn't want the same thing to happen to me. So I went after him and we fought like two crack fiends after the last hit of the pipe. I heard my mother and grandma yelling for us to stop, but I couldn't. For all the times I would hear my mom getting her ass kicked by him, I hit him harder. For every time I heard her telling him to stop, I punched his ass harder. Then I heard my grandma calling my name. That's when I stopped."

Shaun's fists were tight and he was sweating more than when he first walked in. Her heart broke for him. She rubbed his hands and wiped the sweat from his face. Before she could stop herself, she was sitting on his lap, pushing her tongue in his mouth. His hands held her close. Her breathing was long and deep; just like their kissing. This is it. This was the night she was waiting for. Tonight she would give herself to him. Before she changed her mind, she turned and started walking towards her room.

"Are you sure?" he asked her when he reached her room.

She didn't answer him. Instead she grabbed him around

the neck and kissed him, pressing her body against his. She could feel his penis through his pants and then suddenly, she knew this wasn't what she wanted. When his hands reached for her zipper, she moved them. When he reached under her shirt, she tried moving away from him.

"Shaun, no," she whispered, but again his hands were under her shirt. "Shaun, don't," she said as she stepped away from him. He grabbed her and pulled her back against him and again pressed himself against her.

"Shaun… "

His hand clamped over her mouth.

Her mind was whirling around the thought that he was going to rape her.

He pushed her onto her twin bed and climbed on top of her. She kept squirming under him but he was strong. His hands had gotten into her pants and he was pulling them down. She tried closing her legs but he used his for leverage and she did the only thing she knew to do. She began slapping the side of his face, and clawing at his hands like a crazed animal. It seemed as it wasn't making a difference as he got stronger and stronger until she felt something trying to invade her and then she screamed.

"Baby, oh baby. I'm sorry," Shaun started saying.

"Yes, you sure are," she said, sitting up and fixing her clothes.

"Cheryl, I'm sorry. That ain't me, I'm not like him. I'm not."

She jumped from the bed and snatched her pants up and then saw his face.

"Baby, I'm sorry…so sorry…please, this ain't me, this ain't how I wanted our night to be, you gotta believe me."

She looked down at him and felt sorry for him. He had been through enough tonight and she didn't want to talk about what might have happened if she didn't stop him.

"I know it's not you," She said while rubbing his back.

Chapter 10

Cheryl had gotten lost in her thoughts and realized the water was getting cold. After stepping from the shower, Cheryl decided to slide on her little red dress. She found her red heels and was set. She decided that instead of curling her hair, she would snatch it back in a ponytail. If he had wanted to leave then he shouldn't have wanted sex, she thought to herself. She was finally ready and walked downstairs and didn't see Kevin, so she walked towards the kitchen, thinking he might already be outside, but stopped when she heard him in his office.

"Nigga please, she ain't going to find out nuttin', less you tell her."

"Cause I can nigga." she heard him say.

"I'm going to end the game when I get back. I'm tired of all of the bullshit anyway."

A smile came across her face because maybe the sex and all of the nice things she had been doing for him lately, finally made him realize what he had in her. She was happy because she didn't want to share her husband any longer.

"Whateva Nigga, just be on time, and make sure you have all of the documents."

She stepped back into the hallway and went back into the kitchen and waited for him to come in.

"Are you ready?" she said when he finally came in and

put the glass in the sink.

"What; you listening to my conversations now?" he asked.

She turned around, "No, I just got down here and was headed out the door because I thought you were waiting for me."

"Hell, as long as you took, I should have just gone on without you," He said and bumped past her.

"You want me to drive?"

She handed him her keys and he put them on the counter.

"Did I say that? Just come on before I change my damn mind."

"I just thought that since…"

"I didn't ask you, now did I?" he said as he snatched his keys from the hook by the door.

"I just thought you would want to take my truck…"

"Shut up! Goddamn! Can you give it a break? We are taking my car, end of story," he said as he walked out of the door and let it slam behind him.

She set the alarm and walked out into the garage and got in. The music was already turned way up and it gave her an instant headache. She reached over and pushed the knob to turn it down.

"Don't fucking touch my radio."

"It's just that it is a little too loud."

"Well, you could walk," he said as he pushed the remote and the door came up and he backed out.

They rode in silence as her headache got worse.

"Honey, can you please just turn it down a little?" She said as she touched his hand.

He snatched his hand away as if he had been burned by her touch. After about another minute he finally adjusted the sound from the steering wheel.

He finally spoke when she looked at him again. "Look, since I'm going to be gone a few days, why don't you do something for yourself?"

"Maybe."

"Well at least think about it. Why don't you use one of the many credit cards I give you and go get your hair done or something? Maybe get your feet done and your nails."

She tried to keep her mouth closed but she couldn't believe he was acting as if she had all the time in the world to do things for herself.

"Maybe if you were home more and did some of the things with the kids, I would have time to do something, like get my hair done,"

"Look, don't start this shit again."

"What shit? I am only telling you that I don't have time since you are always out and about," She said as she turned her face towards the window.

"Look, just cool down and let's have some fun tonight for a change." He continued driving but she heard him mumbling under his breath.

Then he started talking again, "See when I try and do something nice for your ungrateful ass, you gotta act all snotty and shit."

"Ungrateful? What is that supposed to mean? Just because I say that I wish you spent more time with the kids I'm ungrateful? I am not sure how that equates."

"You know what the hell I mean. I always tell you to go and do some shit for yourself and then you try and turn it around on me. Just forget I said anything."

Sometimes silence is golden, but not in the case of the two of them. Silence from Kevin meant he was fuming and hell was about to be open. He pulled the car into an empty parking lot, and sure enough hell opened up and swallowed her.

He pushed the gearshift into park and leaned over almost into her seat.

"Who the fuck do you think you are? I ain't your mothafucking child. I am a grown man and married to the most selfish bitch I have ever known. I give your ass every goddamn thing a woman wants. A truck; that need I remind you, you don't have to pay for or even worry about putting

31

gas in, a damn house worth more than you could ever hope to make in a lifetime, goddamn credit cards that you don't have to pay for, but miraculously they have no balances every fucking month, and those damn bank accounts with balances any ordinary bitch would appreciate. But do you? You complain every goddamn day. I am so sick of hearing you complain. I don't think you could function if you couldn't complain at least five times a damn day. You are such a selfish, ungrateful bitch."

She lost it. He had hit a nerve by calling her the one thing that she hated the most.

"I am not! I am not! I hate you!" she screamed and suddenly she found herself swinging at him and she became incoherent. Her words rushed from her mouth like open floodgates at the river.

"You call me selfish? You're the selfish one! Always worried about your damn self. No one else! It's always what Kevin wants, what Kevin needs! I ask for simple shit. Like for you to love me! For you to care about me! But you can't do that, can you! If you cared for me half as much as your stupid business, then maybe I wouldn't complain! I hate you! I hate you!"

She tried to open the doors of the car and failed. She knew they were locked and hoped that he would release her from her prison.

"Let me out of here!" she screamed when it was clear that he wasn't going to release her. She turned and saw the anger building on his face and the tears started to fall from her eyes. "Let me out of here!"

"Cheryl! Calm the fuck down!" he yelled back at her.

"I hate you, I hate you, I hate you!" were the only words that she could say.

"Cheryl! Look you need to get a hold of yourself! Stop it!" he said as he grabbed her and then he slapped her.

"Look, you really need to calm the fuck down before I lose my goddamn temper."

"Just let me out of this car, unlock the door," she said

again.

"Cheryl, look, we can talk about this. Let's just go home."

She finally gained enough control to unlock the door herself and climbed from the car and started walking. She didn't know where they were or where she was going, all she knew was that she needed to get away from him.

Kevin caught up to her, spun her around and slapped her hard enough to knock her to the ground.

"Get your ass back in the car or so help me..." he said while standing over her.

She didn't move, but he snatched her up.

"Let me go!" she screamed and snatched away from him and started running. Just as he was about to go after her, he saw headlights turn into the parking lot.

"Cheryl, Cheryl!" he shouted.

She continued to run until she heard music from around the corner. She heard him calling her from behind her but she couldn't stop now. She heard him call her again and this time she heard his feet hitting the pavement behind her.

She half ran half walked as quickly as she could in her five inch heels.

"Cheryl!" she heard him call again and this time she knew he was much closer than he was a few seconds ago.

She rounded the corner and had come up to a little hole-in-the- wall club. She brushed by the people standing in line and tried moving closer but now Kevin was behind her. She felt him grab her arm but she managed to pull away before he had a tight grip.

"Look, Cheryl, if you expect me to keep following you like some dog, you are sadly mistaken." He yelled as she turned around, only separated by three women in line.

"Then stop following me." She said, hoping that someone would come to her defense.

"Look, I am really beginning to lose my patience. You need to stop acting all bitchy and come back to the car." He had finally caught up to her and grabbed her upper arm.

"Don't fucking make me drag your ass back. Now come on and I am not saying it again." He said as he pulled her closer.

Her heart was beating faster but her mind was made up, "Get the hell off of me," she said as she tried to pull away again.

"Stop putting on a show for these people. They could care less that you are acting like this."

"Then stop acting man-ish and take your damn hands off of me."

They were standing face to face by now and the crowd was looking like they had just turned on a soap opera.

Kevin squeezed her arm a little tighter this time, causing her to feel her heartbeat in her hand.

She finally snatched free of him and walked as fast as her five -inch heels would carry her. She finally knew where she was and knew if she could get to the corner, there would be a payphone. At least that was the hope. She could get home and leave him to do whatever he wanted to. She was over this evening and just wanted to be home. She needed to get her life in order and being out here in the dark with no ride home was not getting it. What she really needed to do was to figure out how she was going to go about ending her marriage and making a life for herself.

Chapter 11

High school days

Cheryl woke up and Shaun was sitting in her chair, beside the bed.

"How long you been awake?" she asked as she rubbed her eyes and sat up.

"Not long, maybe thirty minutes."

"What time is it?"

"About ten in the morning. Look Cheryl, I want to apologize."

"Come over here" she said, while stretching and yawning at the same time. "Look, I know things weren't what you expected last night and I didn't mean to lead you on. But let me just say this, when it is the time for us to be together we will know it. I shouldn't have tried to rush it. I guess I just don't want to lose you but I'm ok with waiting and I hope you are too.

"Ok, it won't happen again until you want it to," he said and gave her a slight hug.

"Babe, I gotta go. Gotta make sure my mom is ok," he said as he rose from the chair and put his jacket on.

"Look, call me so I know everything is ok," she said as she walked behind him.

"That's a bet. Love you," Shaun said before hopping off the step and running across the street to catch the bus before it left.

"Love you too," she yelled but he was already on the bus.

For the next four hours she waited for a phone call that never came. She called his friend but he said he hadn't seen him since yesterday. She wanted to call his house but she didn't know what was going on and didn't want to interrupt in case something was happening. Her sister came upstairs and bounced into her room.

"We are going to get something to eat. Wanna come?"

"No." she answered her without looking up.

"Dang, even when ma and 'em ain't home, you still little miss goody two shoes. Ma and them won't even know, good lord, can you not be little miss stuck up for once? Well, your loss. See ya." Angel said.

"Whateva" she said as her sister continued looking at her while she dialed Shaun's number.

"May I speak with Shaun?"

"Who is this?" said the woman who picked up the phone.

"Cheryl."

"Oh, hi baby. Shaun ain't here. He left about an hour ago. Guess he told you about all of the foolishness last night. Good thing he left, cause the police showed up here and carted his foolish father off to the jailhouse. Lucky thing too, cause if I had gotten in there, I would have bust his head wide open with my skillet. But you know, baby, I don't move as fast as I used to, but I still got a good arm. Guess playing those slot machines helps."

Cheryl couldn't help but laugh at the old woman. She was almost 70 years old but was a handful, according to Shaun.

"Anyway, I'll tell him to call you when he gets his skinny ass in here."

"Ok. Thank you," Cheryl said as she hung up, disappointed. He promised to call her and he obviously went home and had time to take a shower, but not enough time to call before he bounced back out of the house. She needed to calm down and not let her imagination get the best of her. He would call when he got a chance. He would call.

She fell asleep but woke up when she heard Angel and Dewayne arguing as always. If they weren't screwing, they were arguing. She decided to call Shaun one more time. After the fourth ring, his mom answered.

"Hi Mrs. Sherry, this is Cheryl, Is Shaun home?" she asked her.

"No, he isn't home. You want him to call you?"

"Yes please." Ok, now he was pissing her the hell off. To get her mind off of him, she cleaned her room, listened to the Angel and Dewayne saga, then went outside and sat on the porch until it got dark. She decided to do something to cheer herself up. Cooking always seemed to do that. Well, that and talking to Shaun but since he was nowhere to be found, cooking would have to do for now.

She sat out all the ingredients for chicken and mashed potatoes and went about cutting up the vegetables for a salad. She felt as though she was a chef, in her own little world, where nothing could go wrong. She baked the chicken to perfection, the salad was done and the potatoes were fluffy, but after all of that, she didn't want to eat so she gathered all of the food and started putting it in plastic containers and stuffing it into the refrigerator. She cleaned up the mess she made and she went into her room.

They always spoke to each other at least three or four times a day on the weekend, and here it was almost eight o'clock and she hasn't spoken to him since he left her house earlier that morning. Where in the world was he?

She finally fell asleep and woke up early Sunday and saw Dewayne leaving. So now the song and dance would begin with Angel, to ensure that Cheryl would keep her mouth closed about the weekend. That was the usual ritual.

Cheryl decided to let her out of her misery before she got knee deep in it, "Look, you don't have to be nice to me. I ain't gonna tell on you."

"Dang, I was just trying to be nice; you don't have to bite my head off," Angel said.

"Well, you aren't normally nice to me, so don't do it now."

"Dang, you need to stop acting all stuck up!" Angel screamed.

"I do not!" Cheryl screamed back at her.

"Yes you do. You didn't even say two words the entire time D was here."

"So… he ain't my boyfriend!" Cheryl said as she got up and went to her dresser and yanked open the bottom drawer.

"You could at least speak," Angel said.

"Didn't want too."

"You are such a bitch!" Angel screamed at her and pushed her against the dresser.

"I am not!" Cheryl said and regained her balance.

"Yes you are! That's why you don't have any friends, because you act like a stuck up bitch all the time!" Angel screamed in her face.

"I do not!"

"Only Dee can put up with your snobbish ass!" Angel screamed as Cheryl tried to move past her.

Angel pushed her again and again as Cheryl kept trying to move away from her.

"Get out of my room!" Cheryl finally screamed while tears streamed down her face.

"Make me," Angle said to her.

"Get out!" Cheryl screamed again and tried to get by her.

Cheryl pushed Angel and this time Angel slapped her across the face and pushed her even harder.

Cheryl was breathing harder and was ready to strike back but she didn't. Instead the tears fell. Angel backed off.

"See what I mean, you won't even stick up for yourself. That's why that dumb nigga treats you the way he does," Angel said as she walked out of Cheryl's room.

She threw herself across her bed. The tears became sobs and she began to think, why was it that she only really had one good friend? Dee was her friend from elementary school and besides, she didn't like the way the other girls carried themselves. Of course Angel didn't care if she was called a slut but Cheryl did. Still what Angel had said, caused Cheryl to cry even more. It felt as if her sister was always being mean to her for no reason and she didn't fight back because that is not what she was taught by her parents. You never fight your family, ever. She turned over and cried until she felt exhausted. She didn't have the energy to get up so she just lay there until she felt her eyelids getting heavy.

She woke up to her dad's voice and although she didn't want to be bothered, she got up and went into the kitchen.

"How was the trip?" she asked while plopping down at the kitchen table.

"It was wonderful." Her mother started, "The wedding was so nice but it was a little cheap. I mean, who really has those stupid fish on the tables at the reception. You could tell it was an after-thought. Who doesn't have flowers for the table? The way they had the buffet line, I started to tell your father to go to the chicken place and get me a chicken dinner. The line was so long that the food was cold by the time we got to the front."

"It was a nice wedding and reception, considering they did it themselves." Her father stopped her mother from speaking.

"Well, you like anything." Her mother scoffed at her dad, "besides as long as you were laughing it up with those drunks, you were as happy as Santa Claus on Christmas.

Her father didn't say anything more. He opted to pour himself a glass of orange juice and pull the refrigerator open. "I see someone has been cooking? Is something wrong?"

"No, just felt like cooking." She said as stared at the phone hanging from the wall, hoping to make it ring. She walked out of the kitchen and headed back to her room after waiting ten minutes but Shaun still had not called.

Monday came and Shaun came bouncing up to her.

"Hey, Babe."

"Hey," she said as he slid his arm around her. It felt good but she couldn't get over the hurt feelings she had.

"What, no kiss?" he said.

"What, no phone call?" she replied.

"Sorry bout that. I didn't go straight home. I went to my uncle's house."

If she hadn't had called and spoken to his mom and grandmother she would have believed that.

"I'm going to be late for class," she said while walking away him.

"Gimme a kiss," he said, trying to pull her back to him but she kept walking.

After class Shaun didn't meet her like he normally did. So much for missing her. Things with this relationship were quickly changing. After about a month of this nonsense; barely seeing Shaun, barely talking to him on the phone, and arguing more and more, she started hearing rumors about Shaun and "some" girl. Normally she wouldn't listen to the rumors but after what she heard she knew she had to talk to him on Monday.

The day started normal enough, that was, until Brenda walked up on her.

"Tell Shaun to call me," Brenda said.

"Call you... what should he call you? A ho?" she said smartly.

"Just tell him what I said," Brenda said as she bumped into her on her way to the cafeteria.

"I ain't telling him nuttin." Cheryl said but she doubted she had heard her since the bell had rang at least ten seconds ago.

"You better," Brenda shouted back as she walked away.

Something about that sent a charge through Cheryl ad

she raced behind Brenda.

"I better do what?" She said.

"You heard me. I didn't stutter did I?" she said snottily. Before she knew what she was doing, Cheryl had her arm ready to throw a punch. Mr. Reeves walked up.

"Is there a problem here ladies? If not, then may I suggest you walk on to your next classes and not forget that you are young ladies?"

Cheryl was angrier than a bear caught in a beehive with no honey. For the rest of the day, she heard that Brenda was talking about her. She didn't really care about that. All she cared about was why Shaun had to call that witch. She would definitely deal with this. Dee was supposed to come to her house today to finish helping her work on their project. Picking her as a partner was probably the wrong move. She was always waiting until the last minute to do her work. Completely lost in thought, she was shocked when Shaun bounced up and asked if he could roll home with her that day, what better ending to a shitty day, than going home with your best friend and your boyfriend.

Shaun and Dee met her at her locker at the end of the day.

"Slow down girl, the bus ain't going to leave you," Dee said while pushing her books into Cheryl's locker.

"Girl, my bus is so crowded that if you don't get on early, you will have to stand the whole ride home."

"I don't mind standing," Shaun said. "As long as I get to stand by my baby." He grabbed Cheryl's hand and kissed her cheek.

As they came upon Cheryl's bus, Cheryl saw Brenda standing by the steps to the bus.

"What the hell she standing there for?" she said, to no one in particular.

As Cheryl passed by her, she purposely bumped into her and kept moving. After finding an empty seat, she let Dee slide in first then Cheryl sat down, then Shaun. It was a tight fit, but as long as she was pushed up on Shaun, it didn't matter. After riding for about ten minutes, she heard

Brenda's voice above all the noise.

"Look at them, acting like they can't be without each other."

Brenda kept taunting them the entire ride. Cheryl was beginning to get very irritated.

Shaun could see Cheryl was getting upset, so he leaned into her shoulder and whispered in her ear.

"Don't even listen to them. Just ignore them."

Then someone started throwing paper.

Dee stood up and turned around.

"Whoever is throwing paper, better stop!"

The back of the bus started laughing and as soon as she sat down, they started throwing paper again. This time Cheryl stood up.

"I guess someone can't hear! Stop throwing the damn paper!" she yelled over the roar of the bus. She looked at Brenda with squinted eyes.

"Don't be looking over here!" Brenda yelled.

"I wouldn't want to go blind" Cheryl shouted back. The bus was laughing hysterically at this point.

"Bitch, sit your bald-headed ass down!" Brenda screamed.

"At least it's my own hair, and not some horse's tail all twisted, tangled, and dry!" Cheryl shouted back.

The bus let out a collective, Ooohh.

"Girl, obviously you don't know who you are messing with," Brenda said, while walking up towards the row of seats that Cheryl occupied.

"Sure I do. A little girl who doesn't know her place and is always in grown folk's bizness," she replied while trying to squeeze past Shaun, but he wasn't going to move.

"Sit down!" the bus driver said while looking in his long bus mirror.

"You lucky!" Brenda said, as she waddled back to her seat. Her short round shape made it easier for her to maneuver around a moving bus.

"Naw bitch! You the lucky one!" Cheryl screamed back.

"You were about to get embarrassed!"

"Babe, sit down," Shaun said, while pulling her arm. "Don't worry about her."

"Yeah Shaun, it ain't me she should be worried about, is it?" Brenda shouted.

"Shut the fuck up Brenda!" Shaun shouted, and miraculously she didn't say another word.

As the bus pulled into Cheryl's development, the bus got louder and louder.

"Take my books," Cheryl told Dee as she pushed them into her friends hands.

"Girl, don't trip. Just ignore her. If she wanted to fight, y'all would have already been fighting."

"Listen to Dee," Shaun said. "Just let it go."

"Let it go?" Cheryl asked, "After she done already embarrassed me? If she comes up to me, I ain't backing down and she better be prepared to get her ass thoroughly kicked."

The bus came to a stop and everyone started getting off. Brenda got up and made her way toward the front of the bus. Shaun wouldn't let Cheryl through, so she just stood there waiting.

Brenda had the advantage and took full use of it. She walked up to her and slapped Cheryl as hard as she could. She then grabbed Cheryl by the hair and pulled her hard enough so that she fell in the aisle and jumped on top of her and started swinging. Cheryl struggled to get to her feet but it was no use. Brenda kept swinging and Cheryl was on the losing end of this girl fight. She tried blocking Brenda's fast moving fists but being on the bottom of the fight was not the best place to be.

Suddenly Brenda was being pulled off of Cheryl by someone and being dragged off of the bus. Cheryl got to her feet and was in a daze. Her eye hurt but her pride was hurt more. Her anger overtook her and she came off the bus and went straight for Brenda. They came together like two angry dogs on the sidewalk. When someone finally pulled them apart, Cheryl had a torn shirt, a bloody lip and scratches on her face.

"Come on here, girl!" Dee said, as she pulled Cheryl towards her house.

"How could you get in a fight, after I told you to let it go?" Shaun said as he pulled her to a stop and was in her face like he was going to fight her next.

"I know you ain't asking me that, after she slapped the taste out of my mouth. I didn't see you asking her no damn questions," she said as she snatched her arm away from him.

They got to Cheryl's house and while they headed downstairs, she went to her room to change her shirt before her mother noticed and brushed her hair. She had a major headache, but looking in the mirror, the scratches she had could be covered with a little bit of makeup or explained away by some 'incident' playing basketball in gym. The inside of her mouth hurt like crazy, probably from when she bit the inside of her mouth, when Brenda slapped her. She joined Dee and Shaun in the basement after speaking to her mother, who was watching television in her room. Dee tried to lighten up the mood and so did Cheryl, but Shaun was in a foul mood and nothing that either of them said made it better.

"I gotta go," Shaun said while jumping up from the chair.

"Do you have to?" Cheryl asked as she walked up the stairs behind him.

He never acknowledged her. He pulled the door open and it was all she could do to call out for him to call her later.

"I'll try," he said as he disappeared around the corner.

Cheryl stood at the door and gave a shrug of her shoulders. She went back downstairs because she didn't have time to wallow in what was becoming her mood of late.

She heard her mom calling her and when she came to the top of the stairs she saw her mom with her arms folded and two police officers standing just inside the doorway.

"Cheryl, this officer says he wants to talk to you about a fight," she said, while eyeing her suspiciously

"Yes, ma'am" Cheryl answered while trying not to look at her.

"Are you Cheryl Book?" he asked.

"Yes."

"Were you involved in a fight today with a...?" he said while flipping open his little notebook. "A Brenda Washington?"

"Yes," she answered again and stole a glance at her mother.

"You were?" she asked with a look of anger on her face.

Without being asked by anyone she said," She hit me first. I was getting off of the bus."

"Was there anyone else involved?" the officer asked.

"No sir."

"Are you sure?" he asked, like he didn't believe her.

"Yes."

"Well, Ms. Washington has some pretty serious injuries to her face."

"We fell while we were fighting, but I didn't notice anything wrong with her when she left. Matter of fact, she was still trying to fight me and my friends walked me home."

"Well, this is more than just scrapes. She will actually need a few stitches," he continued.

She rolled her eyes to the top of her head.

"May I have a look at your hands?" he said. She unfolded her arms and stretched out her arms toward him. "That will be all," he said while writing in his little notebook.

Her mom gave her that look that said, get moving. So she walked back downstairs where she was sure that little miss nosey, Dee, was all up in the conversation. It was obvious to even a blind man that Dee was eavesdropping.

As soon as Cheryl reached the bottom step, Dee started with the questions.

"Girl, what happened? What did the cop want?"

"I don't know," she said while shrugging her shoulders.

Her mom was calling her and she told Dee to start cleaning up their project.

"Look, when I'm done, I'll leave but you better call me as soon as you can. They climbed the stairs and her mother was standing there. Dee opened the door and was stepping out when she said her goodbyes.

"Bye Mrs. Book," Dee said.

"Bye Deidre," her mom said.

As soon as Cheryl had shut the door, her mother was in her face yelling.

"How dare you get in a fight in the middle of the street like a street thug?"

"B-but," she stammered.

"But nothing. I have police coming to my house telling me about things I don't have any idea about!"

"B-but."

"Shut up! You must be losing your damn mind!"

"She hit me first!" she yelled back, as if she had lost her mind.

Cheryl didn't see it coming, but her mother had slapped her just as hard as Brenda had and it stung even more since it was in the same side of her face.

"Who do you think you are talking to?" her mom yelled. "I'm the parent here!"

"But she hit me first!" Cheryl yelled again.

Her mother hit her with a closed fist this time and yelled at her, "You better not let me find out that you were fighting over some boy! Get out of my face!"

"You don't care that she hit me?" Cheryl asked.

"No, I don't! You embarrassed me acting like some stupid bitch in the street who doesn't know the first thing about being a young lady."

"I am a young lady but everybody keeps on picking on me! Always pushing me and teasing me and y'all don't even care!" she yelled at her mother.

Her mother advanced towards her again but this time she stopped.

"Go to your room!" she yelled while walking into the kitchen.

Cheryl was hurt from so many things that had happened in the past few days that when she started to cry it all came rushing back. From Shaun disappearing on her after she didn't sleep with him to her sister hitting her while her parents were gone to now her mother acting like she was the worst person in the world. She didn't think she could take anymore. Maybe it was just better to not fight back. To let people treat you any kind of way because she felt that she was always on the losing end of everything anyway. She lay across her bed and cried until there were no more tears. Her heart was hurting and she didn't know what to do about it.

"Heard you got in a fight today," her dad asked as he walked into her room.

"Yes sir."

"Well, Mr. Dayes called and we have to see him in the morning."

"Yes sir."

"Are you hungry?" her mother asked from just outside her bedroom door.

"No ma'am," she said, not looking up.

"Are you feeling ok?" she asked while walking in and sitting next to her dad on her small bed.

"I feel ok. Just tired," she answered.

"Well, if you don't want to eat you can go back to bed. I will check on you later." Cheryl burst into tears again and her dad rubbed her back and told her it would be ok. He told her that he would check on her later and to stay in bed and be ready to go by seven the next morning for their meeting with the principal.

The phone started ringing and she heard her mother telling Shaun that she wasn't feeling well.

"Oh, really? Oh, ok. I will tell her." Cheryl closed her eyes when she heard her mother coming down the hallway towards her room.

"Cheryl, Shaun just called because he heard about the

47

police coming over. I guess Deidre must have told him. Anyway, he called to tell me what happened. I'm sorry for not letting you tell me."

"It's ok."

Her mother put her hand on Cheryl's head and smoothed her hair away from her face.

"You feel a little warm. Let me check your temperature." Her mom rushed out of the room and Cheryl heard her telling her father that it felt as if she had a fever. When she came back and put the thermometer in her mouth, a minute later it confirmed what Cheryl already knew.

"Yeah, you are very warm. Do you want some water? Is your stomach hurting?"

Whenever Cheryl got upset, her body shut down. This time was no different. Her mother tucked the blankets around her and rubbed her back.

"Just sleep and I'll come back in to check on you in a little while."

As her mother left her room, she heard her father asking about her and her mother told him that Cheryl was just a little worked up about the incident and that she would be ok in the morning.

She woke up and the clock read five in the morning. She had slept all night, so she decided to get a jump on the day and get in the shower. She could hear her mom already in the kitchen listening to her gospel songs on the radio.

"Good morning. Are you feeling better?"

"Yes ma'am" She answered.

"Well, we have to be at school at seven o'clock. Ok," she said.

"Ok," She said as she walked out of the kitchen and into the bathroom.

Chapter 12

Consequences

She walked into the club and needed to sit down to clear her head. She walked to the bar and hoped she could just sit there without trying to get picked up or hit on.

"What can I get you? You look like you are having a rough night," the bartender said.

"I'm sorry. Do I need to order something in order to sit here?" she asked her.

"Yes, but why don't I give you one on the house? What you drinking?"

"Rum and coke please." Cheryl really needed something stronger than that, but that would have to do. "I don't have my wallet, but I promise to come back and give you a tip," She said.

"No need. Just calm down and everything will be ok. Sistas gotta look out for each other," she said.

She seemed nice enough. She was kind of tall, and all the men in the place were clamoring to get to a spot where she could serve them. If Cheryl had to guess, the low-cut top that she wore was the draw. However, she had the widest hips you ever could imagine. Looked like she must have pushed out twins or at the very least, a ten-pounder. She turned around and saw Kevin walking in with a woman on his arm. The woman stood eye to eye with Kevin. She had very round hips but not disproportionate. Her dark hair hung in loose curls around her face and the height of her heel would intimidate most people. She had that air of confidence that a woman who never took no for an answer had. She was also the only woman in the place that had on a skirt long enough to make a man guess what she had underneath of it.

Cheryl turned around but Kevin had already made eye contact with her and started toward her.

"Hey sexy," the bartender said, "Ain't seen you in a minute. Where have you been? Making all that paper I assume."

"Hey yourself," Kevin said, while leaning over and planting a kiss on her cheek.

He turned toward Cheryl, "Hey, I have been looking for you," he said while putting his arm around her shoulders.

Cheryl tried to move away from him but he put pressure on her shoulders with his arm.

"Kevin, please; what do you want?" She asked.

Totally ignoring what she was saying, he continued speaking to her like they were out for an enjoyable evening. "You want something to drink?" he asked her

"No, already got something," She said while holding up her watered down drink.

"Oh."

"Look, just leave me alone," she whispered.

As he leaned down, he angrily whispered, "And who the fuck bought you that?"

"No one did." She answered.

"Why are you lying?" He turned from the bar." Who the fuck in here is buying my wife drinks?" he yelled over the music.

A few men turned around and looked at him and her and then continued with their separate conversations.

"Chill, dude," the bartender said. "I gave it to her on the house. She looked a little upset when she walked in here."

Cheryl got up and started walking towards the bathrooms, near the rear of the club. He tried following, but some chick caught his attention, so he stopped and had to talk to her. Cheryl knew she would go home and then he could meet up with her. She sat at a table in the back and finished her drink. She soon heard him calling her again.

"Cheryl," he said as he sat down at her table. "Look, we have some talking to do, and this ain't the place to do it."

"You said everything you needed to say to me." As she stood to walk away, he grabbed her by the arm. "Get your damn hands off of me."

"You better lower your damn voice and sit down like you have some sense," he said as he tried to pull her back down into the booth.

"I said get your hands off of me!"

He jumped up from the table and was in her face instantly.

"Hey, aren't you Mr. Goldman?" said the tall man standing nearby. "I read the last article on you in Black Enterprise magazine. Man, you got real skills when it comes to marketing. I read that you were expanding. It's good to see a black man like yourself doing things the right way."

"Yeah," Kevin said as he still held firm to her arm. "I do what I do," he said.

"Well, let me give you my card and if you ever need anything, let me know. I have a car service that would probably meet the needs of your company," he said as he pulled out a black leather business card holder and handed him a purple embossed card with bold script writing.

Kevin's grip never loosened so she was still held in his vise grip.

He leaned into her and whispered, "Look, let's just go home. You have caused enough of a scene, don't you think?"

She tried yanking her arm away but he held his grip. "Hey, Kevin. Is that you?" another man asked.

"Man, long time no see," they said as they slapped hands. That was her chance.

She walked off before Kevin could introduce her. She walked outside and was met by a slight mist. Just her luck that she didn't have her purse or her umbrella. She tried her best not to be too emotional but it was becoming harder to do. She walked to the corner and found a phone booth. She dialed Dee's number and started talking before she realized that it was Dee's answering machine.

"Dee, I'm stranded downtown can you come and get me please. I don't have my purse and I need a ride home. I am at The Bottom. Thanks"

She hung up and walked back towards the club. The mist was beginning to chill her but she didn't want to risk going back into the club.

"Excuse me, Miss?" said the gentleman who had spoken to Kevin earlier in the evening.

"Yes?"

"You really shouldn't be standing out here alone. Some of these jokers will get the wrong idea."

"And what idea would that be."

"That a young, attractive woman, is available, if you know what I mean."

"No, I'm sorry. I don't know what you mean. I am not available and I am not looking for anything from anyone. Look, Kevin is still inside if you are looking for him."

"No ma'am. I was heading home, since my buddies think that a good time means hitting on any and everything in a skirt."

"Well, isn't that what you guys do?"

"No ma'am. Well, not me anyway. I like to come out, dance a little, have some nice conversation and something to drink, then head home."

"Well, aren't you special? Look, have a good night," she said as she continued past him and looked down the street. She started shuffling back and forth and wrapped her arms around herself in an effort to keep warm.

"Well, this isn't the best place to stand outside. Can I offer you a ride somewhere?"

"I don't even know you." She said with attitude.

"I'm sorry. My name is Matthew."

"Nice name," she said sarcastically

"Do you have a name?" he asked

"Yes."

"Mind telling me?"

"Why?"

"Cause I introduced myself. Now it is only common courtesy to introduce yourself."

"I didn't ask you to tell me your name. So, consider this as me being rude."

"Wow. Didn't know a woman as fine as you could be so cruel."

"Whatever." She said as she turned her head while rolling her eyes at him.

"Well, the offer stands, Ms. No-name, if I can drop you somewhere, I will."

"No thank you. I called my girlfriend; she should be here in a little while."

"Ok. Well, have a good night," he said as he walked away.

He pulled out his cell and she noticed a limo stop in front of him and he got in.

She started walking back towards the carry out. She went in and asked the person at the counter if she could wait for her ride. The woman behind the counter shrugged her shoulders so Cheryl sat down by the window.

She went back out to the payphone, still kicking herself for leaving her purse in the car but after an hour and trying one more time to ring her friend. Just then a limo stopped, and the back window came down.

"Excuse me. Would you like a ride somewhere?" asked the familiar face.

"No thank you. I thought I said that a little while ago."

"Well, it looks like you still don't have a ride and I don't feel comfortable leaving a pretty young woman out here by herself. You never know who could be lurking in the dark."

I guess you would know because you the one lurking,

she thought to herself but her options had run out and she couldn't see any other way of getting home. She started to walk towards the car.

As she got closer, the driver got out and opened the door and Matthew got out.

"Carl, take her wherever she needs to go. I'll get a ride," he said.

"You don't have to do that. I don't want to put you out." She said as she stepped down from the curb.

"It's no bother. I'll have another drink while I wait." He said as he guided her into the back seat.

"Ms…? What's the address?" Carl asked.

"14400 Albrook Drive, please." she said as she climbed into the back and leaned against the back of the seat.

"If you give me your address, I'll cover whatever extra this is going to cost you." She said.

"No need to do that."

"Are you sure? I don't like owing anyone anything." She said as he stepped away from the car.

"Yes, I'm sure. I got this. Just have a good night." He said.

"Thank you."

"Here, in case you are ever in a jam. You can call them; they are very reliable and prompt."

M & T Car Service. Call us when you want to feel like a star.

MPerry/TWayne/owners

Chapter 13

Cheryl and her parents arrived at the school about twenty minutes early. They had to wait for the principal to finish up with some things before they could see him. They walked in and the principal asked her to tell her version of the story. After telling her side of the story, they asked her to wait in the hall. After about twenty minutes they called her back in.

"The decision has been made that you will be off of the bus for one week," Mr. Dayes said. "You will also need to stay away from Brenda."

"I didn't start it," Cheryl whined.

"Well as far as we can tell you are telling the truth, but we don't know how she sustained such serious injuries. Her mother was ready to press charges because of the endangerment of her daughter and grandchild, but she has since changed her mind. We are asking that you stay as far away from her as possible. Is that too much to ask?"

"As long as she doesn't bother me," Cheryl said with more attitude than she really should have had.

"Well, even if she does, you need to walk away."

"I'm not going to let her hit me."

Mr. Daye's eyes frowned. "It seems like you do not understand me..."

Cheryl interrupted him. "Yes I do. But if she hits me, like she did this time, I am not walking away."

Her dad spoke up. "Surely you don't expect my

daughter to let someone hit her and she not defend herself."

"No, I am not. I am asking that she is not the aggressor." Mr. Dayes responded.

"My daughter was not the aggressor this time. This other girl, who doesn't ride my daughter's bus, rode her bus home and hit my daughter before my daughter had a chance to get off of the bus."

"I understand that, and we have spoken to her about that and she won't be allowed on any bus for at least a month."

After another few minutes of talking, they were free to go. Upon leaving the office, Brenda's mother came walking up to them.

"I just want to apologize for the stupid actions of my daughter. Ever since she found about, well anyway, she has been acting out and I am just glad my grandchild is ok."

"Well, I am sorry it became physical," Cheryl's mother said. "It's just sad that two young ladies were acting like they didn't have home training and settling it with violence."

Cheryl rolled her eyes at her mother for making an assumption, just as she had the day before.

"Are you staying or do you want to go home?" her dad asked her.

"No sir. I already missed three classes today. I would rather stay."

"Ok, see you later then," he said and her parents started towards the parking lot.

"Girl, what in the world is going on?" Dee started the questions as soon as she saw Cheryl.

"Nothing, I just can't go around Brenda and vice versa, and I can't ride the bus for a week. Have you seen Shaun today?"

"Naw, why?"

"I need to talk to him."

"If I see him, I'll tell him," Dee said and they walked their separate ways. As she got her books from her lockers she heard people in the hallway talking about yet another girl being pregnant.

"Can you believe it...her of all people?" said the girl with the braids and pink shirt.

"Ew, no. And who in the hell would want a baby with her. She sleeps with any and everybody." Said the girl with the jeans so tight Cheryl could see her panty line.

"Well, whoever it is; I bet he wished he would have worn a rubber."

She sat in class for a while and kept replaying the conversation in the principal's office over and over in her head. She decided that the one person that knew all there was to know at this high school would be Dee. She knew everyone's business and what she didn't know, she found out.

Cheryl didn't see Shaun for almost a week but then he bounced up to her and wanted to take her to their favorite spot. She was a simple girl, and by her own admission, simple minded at times. She loved walking in the park with him and just holding hands and listening to birds sing their songs. She decided it was now or never.

She steered him over to the park bench and sat on top of it.

"Shaun, have you heard what people are saying about you?"

"Yeah, so what, It's just talk."

"It doesn't bother you?" she said as he sat down in front of her and she put her hands through his hair.

"No, you know how people talk."

"Yeah, but they are saying that you got somebody pregnant. Now we both know it ain't me, so why they saying that?"

"I don't know. Why don't you ask them if you are all concerned?" he said as he turned around and looked up at her.

"Don't be getting all testy with me. I was just asking a question. Damn. Unless you keeping something from me."

"W-what is that supposed to mean." He said as he jumped up from his spot on the bench.

"Nothing. God, can't anybody joke around with you." She said, grabbing his hand and pulling him close to her.

"Not about that!"

"Well, I should ask Dee. She knows everything, then we will go and tell them to stop spreading lies about you."

"What would you do that for? You know Dee is just plain nosey anyway and likes to keep shit stirred up."

"Dang, I was only kidding. Don't bite my head off." Shaun started kicking leaves and looking a little uncomfortable.

"Hey, you know I love you, right?" he said looking up at her.

"Yeah, Yeah."

"No seriously. Right?"

"Yeah."

"Good, just remember that."

"As long as you don't forget it," she said as she poked him in his chest.

"Let's get out of here; do you mind if we stop by my house first?" he asked her as he led her to the car.

"Nope, as long as I'm home before eight, that's fine."

They pulled up to his apartment building and got out and Paul walked up to him.

"Hey, B said to call when you got here."

"Whateva, Nigga," Shaun replied.

"Well, I'm only the messenger. And the message has been told." Paul said, and walked away.

"Who is B?" I asked.

"Nobody."

"Well, nobody wants you to call."

"Yeah, I got that." he said and started toward the door.

They got on the elevator and as the doors closed the smell hit her like a brick upside her head. The urine smell and the dingy carpet were enough to make her move closer to Shaun. The lights in the elevator didn't work so once the doors closed you were in darkness. Luckily it wasn't night yet so it didn't bother her. The people in the building must have taken the stairs all the time at night. They got to his floor and he opened the door and she barely made it in before the door shut.

So much for manners, she thought to herself.

"Baby, I know you must be crazy, to walk up in here and not speak to your grandmamma," she said as Shaun breezed by her on his way to the back.

"Granny, I was just thirsty," he said while walking back into the living room. "I was going to speak." He bent over and gave her a kiss.

"That's better, 'cause I would hate to have to get up out of this chair," she said while swatting at him.

"And do what. Need more oxygen?" He laughed, but Cheryl cringed at the disrespect she felt he had just shown to his grandmother.

"Don't look so serious, baby," the older woman said. "If I thought that boy was serious, I would be whooping his ass right now."

"Grandma, why you always trying to get a look at my butt."

"Boy, I diapered your black ass when you was a baby. The only thing different now is the size...I guess." She laughed.

"Whatever you say grandma," Shaun said as he walked back towards his bedroom. "Cheryl, I'm going to change my clothes real quick. Be right back."

She sat down in the living room, on plastic no less. She thought to herself: What is it with black folks and plastic on the furniture? All it does is make the furniture look more dingy once the plastic turns yellow. His grandmother was watching an old black and white movie. She could have at least offered her something to drink. She guessed she wasn't like most grannies.

"Baby, you can go on back. That boy will be forever if you don't hurry him along."

She walked back into his room and he had on his jeans

and shoes, but no shirt. She finally saw him as most girls did. He was the color of a Hershey's bar, had a flat stomach, muscular arms, and a short haircut.

"Grandma wouldn't think you were such a nice girl if she saw you now," he walked up to her and kissed her on her neck and face.

"Oh really, what would she think if she saw this." She said as she kissed him back with lust.

"Babies, I don't hear no talking going on in there."

"Yes grandma," he yelled back.

"Hey, I want to give you something." He walked over to his dresser and came back with a black opal ring.

"This is my grannies. She told me to give it to whoever I wanted to spend my life with." He put it on her right hand, middle finger.

"You know that's the wrong hand." She said

"Dang, why can't you just take it? God, why does it have to be on the right finger, I gave it to you; ain't that enough?" he asked as he dropped her hand and walked over to his chair.

"I'm sorry. I just thought you should know that if you want to get married, you need to ask me first," she said walking over to him.

"Look I know. Can you let me just be the man for once and stop trying to be so damn bossy. God! Now I see what my dad was talking about."

"What does that mean?" she said with her hands on her hips.

"Just that…well sometimes a woman gotta let a man be a man and stop trying to be the woman AND the man."

"What! That is just stupid." She said as he walked away from her. "Besides I was only making a point. You don't have to bite my head off about it."

"Whatever." He grabbed his shirt from the chair and walked out of his room.

"See you later, Granny. Tell Ma I will be back around ten."

"Ok, be careful," she said as the door closed.

They got outside and there stood Brenda.

"Hey Shaun, wait up," she called as she breezed past Cheryl. Shaun acted like he didn't hear her, and kept walking.

"I know you heard me. Oh, sorry. I guess you have to walk your dog first," she said as she got closer to them.

"I got your dog, bitch," Cheryl said while walking towards her.

Shaun grabbed her arm. "C'mon, I thought you weren't supposed to be around her."

"She better keep her damn mouth shut or I will shut it for her."

"Shaun, you better come see what I want, unless you want everybody out here to know your biz-ness," Brenda said with her head rolling around like it was about to come off.

With that, he turned and walked towards her. Whatever he was saying to her had her about to cry. He wouldn't let her get a word in whenever she tried talking. He walked back over to Cheryl, grabbed her hand and started walking.

"What did she want?"

"Nothing."

"Then why in the hell did you go over there then?"

"What's with the million questions?"

"Cause, I want to know why she calling you out."

"Look, just leave it alone."

She snatched her hand from his. "I will not! Why can't you just tell me?"

"Cause it ain't none of your business."

"Like hell it ain't! You are my business!" She said, acting just like the girls she didn't want to be like.

"Look, don't ask me nothing about her."

"Then maybe I'll just ask her."

"Look, just leave it alone; don't give me the third degree. Let's just go to the movies like we planned."

"Not until you answer my question and tell me what that

bitch wanted."

"Look, you don't have to keep calling her names. Let's just go."

"Did I just hear you right? You are defending her fat ass!"

"Hell no."

"Then just tell me."

"Tell you what? Ain't nothing to tell."

"You are such a liar!"

"What!"

"You heard me. Obviously you had something to say to her and now you all mad at me for asking. I think its best that I go home."

"For what?"

"Because I don't feel like going anywhere."

"Damn, you sure know how to spoil a fun day."

"No, I didn't spoil anything. All you had to do was answer one damn question, but you would rather take up for that bitch instead of answering it."

"Look, maybe I do need to take you home since you are all irate!"

"Good."

They got into his car and rode in complete silence. When he pulled into her driveway, she got out and slammed the door. Before she had walked away from the car he was out of the driveway and down the street. She stood there until she couldn't hear his muffler anymore.

Chapter 14

She slipped off her shoes when she went in the house so she didn't wake anyone up. If she could put off the drama until morning she would. She knew there would be plenty of it and she just hoped she could get some sleep before it happened. She noticed that she had forgotten to blow out the candles and that would cause another argument, since he hated for candles to burn when they were out. At least he was asleep so she crept into the room.

With shoes in hand, she got into her bedroom but bumped into the chest at the foot of the bed.

"Crap," she whispered and grabbed her toe.

"If you turn on some mothafuckin' lights, you wouldn't be bumping into shit," Kevin said.

"Why are you standing in the dark? If you were up, then you could have turned on a light," she whispered.

"My house, I can stand in the dark if I want to. Where in the fuck have you been? It's after one in the morning."

"Right where you left me," she said.

"Left you? You mean where you decided to stay and chat it up with all the men in the club."

"No I wasn't. The only reason I was stuck was because you decided that I wasn't pretty enough to take anywhere. So I decided that I should let you enjoy your night without me," she said as she walked past him towards her bathroom. "Besides the woman that was hanging all over you, that trick is probably right up your alley."

"Slow your roll. I don't think she would appreciate being called a trick," he said as he walked behind her.

"Well, I will damn well call her whatever I want."

"You really need to stop. She is a business associate."

"Oh, is that what they call themselves nowadays?"

"See, that's your fucking problem, always jumping to conclusions. You need to check yourself."

"No, you are the one who needs checking."

"You always are accusing me of sleeping around." He had cornered her near the closet.

"Cause you are!" she screamed.

"Look, I am not in the mood to hear this shit again. I asked you a goddamn question, where have you been?"

"Well, I am not in the mood to hear your fucking lies again, just don't expect me to keep putting up with it either."

"And what the fuck does that mean?" he said as his arm came up to the wall behind her.

"It means, don't expect me to keep putting up with it. I am well aware that you gotta be sleeping with someone else, because you barely touch me anymore and when you do, you act like you doing me some sort of a favor."

"You lucky I touch your ass at all, I don't touch you anymore because you aren't attractive to me anymore!"

"Oh, like you're my apple pie," she half laughed.

"Yeah Cheryl, real mature. You act like you are eighty fucking years old. You walk around here like a fucking rag-a-muffin. You wear the ass ugliest clothes I have ever seen. You shop at the thrift store like some women shop at Macy's. You never get your hair done anymore. I am so sick of your hair in a ponytail, I could scream. I am embarrassed for you to even come down to the office because you look like something that the cat dragged in. Just sleeping with you makes my stomach crawl. It just ain't no reason for this shit! You could do better if you wanted to."

She slapped him harder than she thought possible and he slapped her back immediately.

She tried moving past him but his hand prevented her from moving away.

"Move Kevin, I'm tired," she said trying to squeeze by him.

He grabbed her by the arm and shoved her back against the wall. His hand met the side of her face and she saw stars for an instant. She felt as if her face were on fire. He then grabbed her by the throat and pinned her against the wall.

" Ah no…you want to hit me, you bitch…you did that shit earlier and I should have kicked your fucking ass then, but I didn't. Now, oh yeah, now I'm going to deal with you properly." He slapped her twice more.

"Kevin, stop it! I'm sorry. Please just let me go to bed," she screamed as she struggled against his massive frame.

This time the slap sent her to her knees. He pulled her up to him and shoved her against the wall.

"You want to try again? Now answer my goddamn question. Where the fuck were you?"

He slapped her again and sent her to her knees. He yanked her up by her hair and swung her around to him. "Answer me!"

"I've been trying to get home!" she shouted.

"Wrong, if you were, you would have been home hours ago!" He slapped her again, "I am your husband, and don't forget it! You come in here all hours of the night, in a limo no less, and question me about who I am fucking. The better question should be; who did you fuck tonight to be brought home in a limo?"

She let the tears fall.

"Who was it?"

"Nobody!" She screamed.

"I don't fucking believe you!" He yanked her dress up and pushed his hand down her into panties.

"Stop it!" she screamed and tried pushing away from him.

"Didn't I fucking tell you?" He said as he slapped her hard once more. "Answer my fucking question. Who the fuck brought you home?"

"Kevin, please!"

"Wrong answer!" He shoved her to the floor, and then tore at her dress.

"Stop it!"

"Did you tell him to stop?"

"There is no him!"

"Sure there is!"

"Stop Kevin, you're hurting my arm." He had pinned her arms above her head.

"Oh, poor thing. You better tell me the truth or so help you, you will regret it."

"Kevin please stop!" He yanked her panties down.

She struggled against him and continued screaming until he covered her mouth.

Suddenly the phone rang. After three more rings he snatched it from the cradle.

"What!" He stood up and took two steps away from her. "What! Yeah, yeah nigga, they are on top of the desk on top of the purple folder." He hung up and looked down on her. He came over and knelt down. "You are lucky. You just remember if you ever think about doing that shit you did tonight, you will be sorry. If I ever find out that you slept with someone else, your ass is mine. You'll be sorry. Do I make myself clear?"

She didn't answer fast enough, so he yanked her up by the hair and put his hand around her throat.

"I said, do I make myself clear?"

She nodded her head rapidly.

He pushed her away from him and she stood there until he left the room. Suddenly her bladder was full and she rushed into the bathroom. As she sat there, the tears flowed down her face and then the sobs racked her body. She heard the bedroom door open and she grabbed a towel from the rack and covered her mouth. He didn't' like to hear her crying. Not because he felt sorry for her, but because "it got on his nerves." After ten minutes she calmed herself enough to stand and pull the washcloth down and ran the cold water. She placed the cold cloth against her face and thought she let out a soft "ah" as the coolness felt absolutely wonderful against her burning skin. She opened the door and saw him sitting there with a glass in his hand. She walked by him and then stopped.

"Kevin, the bar offered free rides, so I accepted. I'm sorry."

She knew that the apology was a lie, in her heart and in spirit but she had to get him calm before his business trip the next day. He couldn't function when he was stressed. She knew he needed to be at his best. "You have an early flight, why don't you get to bed."

She pulled the covers of the duvet back and he stood quickly, causing her to react. He unbuckled his pants and started undressing. She left the room and headed downstairs to make sure that he had packed everything and that his coffee was set. He liked two things for his trip: his favorite coffee mug and the strongest coffee possible. She pulled out the mug and went to the pantry and pulled the container of bold roasted coffee beans from the shelf. She readied the pot and set the timer for 5:00 AM. While she did this she continued crying, not for what happened but because of what she was doing. She was still making sure that he had everything he needed and yet he never did the same for her. She continued crying and then he called from upstairs.

"Cheryl, look, I'm sorry. You know I don't mean to hit you but you know you shouldn't piss me off, right?"

She got up and started towards the stairs, she saw him in the darkness standing at the top, "I know, I am sorry, it won't happen again."

"You know I have to get up early and can't sleep without something beside me. So come on upstairs and get in bed."

"I will in a minute."

"Sorry, didn't hear you." He took one step down.

"Sorry, I was in the middle of fixing your coffee for tomorrow. I'll be up in one minute," she said meekly.

Chapter 15

Cheryl hadn't heard from Shaun since the day in the park and that was almost two weeks ago. He hadn't been to school and when she asked Paul about him, he acted as if he was being questioned by the police and needed a lawyer. She wanted to call him so many times but her stubbornness wouldn't let her. Now she was beginning to get worried about him. It wasn't like him to miss this much school unless something was wrong.

Cheryl made up her mind on the way home, she was calling him.

"Hello, is Shaun home?"

"Didn't I tell you to stop calling here? If he wants to talk to you, he will call you." It was his mother's voice but she had never acted this way towards her before. She decided to call right back.

As soon as someone picked up the phone, she started talking. "Hello, Ms. Mason is Shaun home?"

"Hello sweetie. No, he isn't home. I will tell him to call you."

"Thank you. I'm sorry I bothered you."

"Chile, you ain't bothering me."

"I just called and..."

"Oh sweetie, I thought you were...well anyway, I will definitely tell him to call you as soon as he walks in the door."

"Thanks." That was the end of that call but Cheryl

wondered who Ms. Mason was talking about and why was she so angry?

Shaun called her an hour later.

"Hey."

"Hey yourself. Where you been?" she immediately asked.

"Why?" he answered with a little too much attitude for her taste.

"Cause you haven't called."

"You ain't called me either," he answered back.

"Well the last time we saw each other, you had attitude," she replied.

"I wonder why," Shaun said.

"I ain't done nuttin to you."

"Yeah, you go with that," he said.

"No, really Shaun, you act like this is my fault. You were the one tripping!"

"What you need to do, is stop calling her names."

"And again, you are defending her." Cheryl's voice came out as a high pitched squeal.

"Look, we haven't seen each other in a minute, is this how you want to spend it? You always gotta be pushing my buttons. Damn. Look why don't I come and get you and we can go somewhere and talk."

I have something to do," she said. Now she was the one with attitude.

"Oh, ok, I ain't going to beg you to be with me."

"I didn't ask you to beg me. I called your house and your mom thought I was someone else that keeps calling you. Who is she?" she blurted out.

"Who?"

"The person that keeps calling you."

"I don't know."

"Oh is that the person's name," she pressed.

"Let me call you back."

Just like that, no goodbye, see you later, nothing. She held the phone for almost five minutes before calling back and when she talked to his mother, she said he left.

Cheryl was angry but she had chores to do and she didn't need her mother being on her case even more than she was for the past month.

The doorbell rang and she bounced down the three steps to the door and opened it to Shaun who stood there looking nervous.

"Well I hope this means you came over here to tell me the truth," she said as she folded her arms without letting him in.

"Tell you what truth? I don't know what you are talking about." He said while rocking back and forth.

"How about we start with who is calling you and why you hung up on me?"

"Look, can we go somewhere and talk?" he said while reaching out to touch her.

"About what, just tell me now"

"Not here where everybody can be in our business." he said looking around.

"Just tell me, I am still on punishment since the whole fight thing and I ain't asking my mother for nothing," She said while looking over her shoulder.

"Look, just ask her, tell her you have some homework you need to do with some of those smart ass kids you hang out with all the time. She'll believe that."

"Look whatever you need to tell me, you better be doing it while you are standing here because I can't go."

"Look…can you at least come outside?"

"Let me tell my mom first."

She came back and plopped down on the porch and Shaun was still standing.

"So answer me this, are we still boyfriend and girlfriend?" she asked, looking up at him.

"Yeah."

"Ok, so why are you acting like you can't talk to me?"

"Look, um…"He started shifting back and forth. "Things just ain't working out right now…"

She cut him off, "what does that mean, not working out

right now. Between us? Look, you need to stop stalling and get to talking. Let me just tell you what I know. Ever since that night a while ago, we have been arguing more and more. You barely come over any more. You hardly ever call me."

He sat down beside her and said, "You know I love you right?"

"Right."

"So no matter what, you won't leave me?" he asked

"Well, unless you got another girlfriend, no I won't leave you."

"Well."

"Wait, do you have another girlfriend?" she said and jumped from the porch."

"No, nothing like that. But you know since that fight, you been different. I never thought I would see you be so mean."

"What does that have to do with anything?"

"Everything."

"Look, you didn't have anything to do with us fighting. That was going to happen anyway."

"I just figured that if I came home with you that day..."

"So that's the only reason you came home with me that day?" She was getting louder and louder.

"No, not the only reason. But when I heard y'all might fight, I just figured if I was there she wouldn't."

"She wouldn't what?"

"Then she wouldn't want to fight and then you was acting ghetto and like someone I didn't even know."

"What? Are you kidding me right now? She started it. What was I supposed to do? Just let her kick my ass and do nothing?"

"Let me finish. Y'all started fighting and afterwards you acted like nothing happened."

"I was supposed to let her just slap me and do nothing? I don't think so."

"But you acted like you didn't care if she was hurt."

"You have got to be kidding me. I didn't give a rat's ass whether she was hurt or not. Was I supposed to ask her if she was? She is the one who started it, so she got what she deserved. I know you are not trying to tell me that you cared if she was hurt. I know you are not going to stand there and tell ME that! What about me. I'm your damn girlfriend, not her."

"No, not really."

"Not really? What in the hell does that mean?"

"What I mean is. Look I made a mistake and I'm sorry for it."

"Ok, I do not understand." At this point she was getting frustrated. Shaun was never a good speaker especially if he got nervous but now was not the time that she felt like dealing with that.

He continued, "You have been so good for me and I love being around you. I would never do anything to hurt you."

"What does that have to do with the fight? Jeez, you are rambling Shaun."

"You remember when I came over to your house that night."

"Yeah, so I knew that would come back up. So you were mad."

"No, I wasn't mad, but something happened when I got home."

"What? Was your mom hurt? Was your dad still there?"

"No. Nothing like that. After I left your house. I went home and took a shower and left."

'I know."

"How?"

"I called and your grandma said you had left out again."

"Yeah, so I hooked up with Kenny and Kevin. Well they had weed and beer and I went down with them and started smoking and drinking. Well, they had some girls come over and after a while, they went in back with the two of them."

"Eww, they are just nasty" she said out loud.

"Yeah, well, I don't know what happened back there.

73

Anyway, I was left out there with the other girl and we started talking and she was a nice person. She ain't like people say she is."

"Ok. So."

"So, we were talking and then we started to kiss and..."

She didn't let him finish, "Beep, beep, and beep, back the truck up! Started kissing? You kissed some chic you didn't even know?"

"Yeah," he said matter of factly. "And…"

"And! And! There's an and?" she was now louder than she knew she should be because Mrs. Johnson stopped digging in the dirt and turned towards her, "Don't tell me there is more!" she said, as she sat down hard beside him.

"Yeah there is," he said while looking down at his shoes. After hesitating, he finished, "I slept with her."

"WH- What the fuck did you just say to me?" She put her hand over her mouth as if to stop the other curse words from coming out. She jumped up and paced back and forth in her front yard.

Shaun stood and tried to grab her hand, "Cheryl, wait. Calm down, ok let me explain."

"What is there to say? You slept with someone else and you expect me to sit here while you explain?"

"Cheryl, calm down a minute."

"Calm down! You expect me to calm down when you tell me you slept with someone else. So after I wouldn't sleep with you, you went to the first girl who would spread her legs open for you."

"It was an accident."

"An accident? No an accident is a car hitting another car. Your penis going in somebody is not an accident."

"Lower your voice," he said while looking around.

"Screw you Shaun. Oh I forgot, you already did that. With…who?"

"What?"

"Who? Who is she?"

"It doesn't matter," he said while turning away from her.

"Like hell it doesn't. Let's think of who it could be. Angel? No she just had a baby and that would be too low, even for her. Dee? Naw, she my girl. Shelly? Nope, she got a boyfriend for the moment. So who is it?" Shaun's face was tighter than a fat woman's girdle. He whispered something. "What did you say?"

"Brenda." He said.

"Brenda what?"

"It was Brenda. I'm sorry," he said, but all she could see was his mouth moving. Everything around her stood still.

"You sure are. You are a selfish sonofabitch. I can't believe you would sleep with someone who has slept with almost the entire boy population of our school."

"Cheryl, wait. Let me just explain," he said as he grabbed her arm.

"Explain what? That when I wouldn't give it up, you call up ol' girl and she was more than willing?" she said and pushed him away.

"It wasn't like that."

"Oh, it wasn't? Then tell me how it was."

"Cheryl, it wasn't planned. It just happened. We were talking and then we…"

"Spare me the gory details." As she walked away, her anger got the better of her and she whirled back and slapped him.

"She's pregnant!" he said as if her slapping him had made the words fall from his mouth.

"Get away from me," she said to him as he tried holding her.

"Cheryl, wait. Let me explain."

"Explain what? How long have you known that she was pregnant?"

"Since y'all got in the fight. That's why I didn't want y'all fighting, because she knew she was pregnant."

"So it just happened that you came to my house that day. But really, so the only reason you came was so we didn't fight? You were protecting her? You make me sick!"

"I wasn't protecting her. I just didn't want you to be

fighting that's all." She continued walking and Shaun caught her by the arm.

"Get your damn hands off of me!"

Mrs. Johnson stood up and asked, "Are you ok over there?"

"Yes, he was just leaving," she said as she stepped inside of her doorway.

"No, I wasn't," he said as he put his arm between the door and the jamb.

"Yes you are. Get out of here, you sorry sonofabitch! You couldn't wait for us to be together, you just had to have some ass. No wonder you didn't want to have sex with me, because you had already fucked that bitch! Then you have the nerve to give me this ring!" She tossed the ring towards him and it flew past him into the grass.

"Cheryl, please don't do this, I love you, not her!" Tears were rolling down his face.

"Well, you sure as hell don't love me, because if you did you wouldn't have slept with her!"

"Baby please," he whined.

"Don't fucking call me that! I am not your baby; besides Brenda is having that for you! I hate you."

"Please," he started and pulled her back out the door.

"No, I hate you. I will never ever forgive you." He grabbed her and pulled her into his arms.

"Cheryl, please," he pleaded as tears were forming puddles in his eyes. "I never meant for this to happen."

"You're damn right. You never meant for me to find out that you got somebody pregnant."

"I didn't do it on purpose."

"I don't care how you done it, It's over. When you think about me, stop. Don't call me; don't come up to me at school. Forget that we were ever a couple, cause I sure will. When you see me, act like I'm a stranger. You had my heart Shaun, and you, not Brenda, broke it into a million pieces."

Cheryl felt like time was standing still.

Let Me Just Say This

Chapter 16

She went back into the kitchen and started wiping the countertops and putting the dishes away from the dishwasher. This was a habit she developed when she was younger to deal with stress. She wanted to have control over something and cleaning was it. She could scrub as hard as she wanted to and not worry about breaking anything.

After getting his bags downstairs, she decided to check them to make sure he had packed everything. Ok, well maybe she was just being nosey. She unzipped his carry-on bag and marveled at the wonderful taste he had in clothes. Every suit had the coordinating socks, hankie and tie. She saw a new suit from Brooks Brothers and she saw the shirt with socks, hankie and tie bundled together.

She then saw the bag that carried his four bottles of cologne, electric shaver, mustache trimmer, tweezers, soap, two bottles of lotion, Vaseline, toothbrush, toothpaste, dental floss, and condoms.

She had passed them over so quickly she didn't think they could have been what she thought they were but when she turned over the box, it confirmed her thought. He had an unopened box of condoms.

She held the box in her hand and stared at them. To her surprise she was calm and after checking his other luggage, she put it all by the door in the kitchen, which led to the garage. She went back upstairs and laid out his usual "traveling" clothes. Silk shirt, with no-wrinkle brown pants and brown loafers. She made sure that everything in the bathroom was laid out so that he didn't have to look for anything. She finally grew tired and crawled into bed beside him. He moaned her name and drew her close. She held her breath to stop the tears and then let her eyes close as the tears began.

Kevin awoke to the smell of coffee. At least he was not in a jail cell.

That was nice of her, he thought. She could be thoughtful at times.

Kevin walked in the bathroom and saw his clothes hanging there. Why can't she be the woman I married? The one who gave a shit about what she looked like, the one I would rush home to and make love to for hours. The one who was confident and self-assured. He walked out of the bathroom and saw the note:

Hope you have a productive trip. Be safe.

Hmm, that was the first time she hadn't made little hearts or smiley faces on her note.

He walked downstairs and filled his travel mug with hot coffee. He noticed his luggage already by the back door. A smile crept on his face.

Cory knocked at the door.

"What up Nigga? You ready?" Kevin looked at his watch.

"Damn, am I late? You ain't neva been on time."

"Whateva Nigga, just come your slow ass on. Besides the quicker you get to the airport, the quicker you get to see her. She already there, she hit me on the cell this morning."

"Shh Nigga, Cheryl is right upstairs."

"Cut yourself shaving?" Cory asked while turning Kevin's head to the side. Kevin slapped his hand away.

"What?"

"You got a cut on your face."

"Probably," he said while walking out into the garage. "Be right back," he yelled to Cory as he sprinted back into the house.

He took the stairs two at a time. He opened the door and saw her laying there with just her bra and panties on. As he kneeled down beside her, he noticed a bruise on her neck. As he looked further down, he noticed more bruises. He nudged her and she jumped away from him.

"Hey sleepyhead. Look, I'm sorry about last night. You know I would never intentionally hurt you. I will call you later. Ok. Look, when I get back we will go away for a few days."

He tried to kiss her. She turned over and offered no response.

"You are going to miss your flight," she said dryly.

As Kevin walked back downstairs he took out his phone. "Yeah, twelve will be fine. Thanks. Make sure you hook them up like I know you can."

"Everything ok?" Corey asked as he got into the car.

"Yeah," Kevin replied but he couldn't shake the nagging feeling he had on the inside that something had definitely changed last night between him and her.

Chapter 17

She climbed on her bed and cried as if the world had crumbled beneath her and she was in the pit of hell. She cried even harder when she thought of all the plans they had. She was saving herself for him and there he was; giving his away to the first pair of open legs. Maybe Angel was right. Almost as if she had heard her thoughts, Angel walked in without knocking.

"Can't you knock?" she said through tears.

"What's wrong?"

"Nothing."

"So you just sitting here crying just because?"

"Yep" she said, not bothering to look at her.

"No you are not. Now tell me. Did somebody do something to you?" she asked.

"Shaun." Cheryl said, looking up at her sister.

"What, damnit will you stop talking in riddles?" her sister said.

"Shaun did something."

"What did he do?"

"He's having a baby." Her whimpers became full sobs

"Who told you that? You know you can't believe everything you hear," her sister said.

"Oh no? Not even when it was him that told me?"

Angel sat down on her bed. "Ok, just let me say this. Eww. What is wrong with him?"

"I should have done like you said. I should have just

given him some. Instead he went and got it from somebody else." She cried harder into her pillow.

"No you shouldn't have," She said while rubbing her sister's back. "You believe in why you didn't sleep with him and that's a good thing. Look, you will eventually find somebody that will appreciate you waiting and he wasn't that cute anyway. You can get plenty where he came from. Ok."

Cheryl turned over and continued to cry. She didn't want anyone else she wanted him and now she knew there was no way she was going to have him.

Chapter 18

By the time Kevin and Cory got to the airport, Kevin's mind was on something else, well, someone else. They checked their luggage and headed for the gate they would depart from. As they walked up, he spotted her. Damn, every time he saw her, it was like he was a nervous teenage boy going on his first date.

"Man, you got it bad." Cory said.

"Got what," Kevin answered.

"Man, even a blind man could see you got feelings for her."

"And how do you know that?"

"Look, it's like I'm walking beside the goddamn sun. I'm just glad I got my sunglasses with me," Corey said as he pulled his dark glasses back into place.

There was no denying it. Kevin did have it bad for her. He had never intended to fall in love with her. He could remember when he knew he had fallen hard. He and Cheryl had yet another stupid argument. So he called her just to talk since they had gotten to be friends. They talked for hours about the argument he had with his wife and he told her how he could talk to her so much easier than Cheryl. He told her that he liked how she understood everything he was trying to do and how he worked so hard for a few years, so he wouldn't have to work the rest of his years. He had asked her to meet him for drinks and she agreed. As they sat and talked he told her how his heart was becoming involved with her in more than just a friendship way and she told him she felt the same. He actually confessed to her how he felt the very first time she walked into their offices three years ago.

"Hey man, the agency is sending over one more candidate for the position." Cory started shifting folders on the desk until he found the one he was looking for. "Umm, her name is Rebecca Hardy. She graduated from North Carolina A & T, with a degree in business management. She should be on her way."

Kevin rolled his eyes before he spoke. "Well, I hope she ain't a waste of our time. We told them what we wanted and they keep sending us these goddamn kids who don't know shit about what they want out of life, let alone know how to run an office."

Corey pushed the papers across his desk, "well after I got off da phone with them I think they got the message that if they keep sending us crap, we would pull our temp contract with them."

Kevin jumped up from his seat. "You did what!"

"Look, calm down, it was just a threat. They have to know you mean business."

"They have been cool when it comes to giving us temps for the summer, so don't go fucking that up for us." Kevin flopped back down into his seat.

Kevin liked Cory's business attitude, but sometimes he would get a little beside himself with power.

Kevin took a sip of coffee, "so after your little threat, what did they say?"

"That's when they told me about this Miss Hardy chic. They said she had recently lost her job with a big internet company and that she was one of the most desirable temps," Cory said while walking towards the door.

"Well, if she is so damn desirable, why didn't anyone offer her a job yet?" Kevin wondered aloud.

"Same thing I asked, they said something about her being very selective."

"Great just what we need, an uppity white woman," Kevin said, while sucking his teeth.

They were interrupted by the phone. Kevin walked towards the desk and picked up Cory's phone.

"K & B Alliance, Kevin speaking. Yes, good afternoon Miss Hardy. My partner was just informing me about our meeting this afternoon. Yes. We are on the same block as the new Starbucks. We are two doors down, take the elevator to the third floor, and then pick a door." Kevin let out a sly laugh. "Yes, exactly. We are the third floor. Ok. See you in an hour."

Kevin was proud that within the span of five years his company was able to afford to lease the entire floor and of course with the help of the owners, they were able to come to an agreement on how the floor could be renovated to make everyone happy. They ended up having all of the walls knocked out. They always said that if they were blessed with their own space; they would knock out the walls and make two of the offices the same with enough space for a reception area. Same amount of windows, doors and floor space. They went in 50/50 and that is the way it would stay. The only distinction would be how they decorated their offices. Cory, well he was your typical bachelor. Black and leather everywhere. Whereas, Kevin had more of an Italian flair, with clean lines, as the decorators would say. They didn't bother with the uppity white woman, which was suggested, for interior design. They went with their own taste. They allocated one office for their mutual secretaries. Black (Cory) had found his secretary a while ago, but Kevin, well he was very picky. They agreed that "Barbie" wasn't office manager material and besides she wasn't the brightest bulb in the socket, although she suited Black well. Kevin knew that Black "occasionally" got with her and he didn't care as long as they were discreet and it didn't affect his work. She wasn't the best secretary, but Black was blinded by the blond.

"Well Mr. Know It All, what do you think?" Cory asked.

"Well." And then came the look.

"What's the look for?" Black asked.

"What look?"

"The look that says, I will interview her, but she won't have a job."

"Cause I ain't hiring no white woman to be my office manager. I said it before, and I mean it; I will not be like a lot of these black men who make it to the top and then hire a bunch of white people to run things for them."

"And how do you know she is white."

"Come on now. How many black women do you know with the name Rebecca?"

"About as many as you know named Cheryl." Cory said.

"Nigga got jokes."

"All day. Besides, ain't no different than how you talk."

Kevin raised an eyebrow. "And what does that mean?"

"Oh, you heard me Mr. White America."

"Whateva nigga."

Black got up and walked toward Kevin. "The only time I know you still my boy is when we hanging out. You talk so fucking proper it ain't even funny."

"It's called proper English, my brotha."

"It's called, white America nigga." They both started laughing.

"You want me to sit in on the interview?"

"And you know this. Have Barbie give her the pre-interview sheet and then bring her in."

"I will tell Ashley."

As Kevin got up and walked to the window overlooking downtown, he ignored Cory's sarcastic remark. Kevin knew Cory didn't like him calling her Barbie, but she was the typical white girl. Bleached blond hair, big ass tits, and lots of lip gloss, earrings in her nose, tongue, not to mention she loved herself some black men.

"Might as well see if Miss Hardy can fit in especially with a woman who has been here more than two years. Who knows she might become Barbie's, I mean Ashley's boss."

"Cool, I'll let her know." Cory said as Kevin walked out

the door.

"You do that."

Chapter 19

The phone began ringing. Cheryl acted like she didn't hear her mom calling her. When her mom came to her room, she closed her eyes.

"Shaun, Cheryl is asleep. I will tell her to call you when she gets up." Cheryl continued to lie on her bed until she couldn't take it anymore. She was too curious for her own good so she got up and went into her mother's room.

"Shaun called, and wants you to call him." Just the sound of his name made her angry. "And why are you rolling your eyes at me?"

"Sorry."

"Are you and Shaun ok?"

"Yeah, I will call him later," she said as she walked out of her mom's room and into the kitchen. The phone rang but she didn't bother answering it. She figured it would be him and she would deal with that when the time.

"Oh yes, she just walked in the kitchen I think. Cheryl pick up the phone, its Shaun."

She snatched up the phone with no intention of staying on the line. She had already changed her mind about talking to him.

He started talking immediately. "Cheryl don't hang up. Just listen. Nothing like this has ever happened before. It was an accident and I will always regret that it happened."

She cut him off immediately. "No, you are only sorry because you got caught. For all I know you have done this before and I have been too damn blind and dumb to see it."

"No it hasn't. You gotta believe me."

"No, you have that all wrong. My grandmother says all I gotta do is grow old and die."

"Babe, please. Let's talk about this some more."

"No! In case you didn't understand earlier. I don't want you calling me, talking to me at school, thinking about me or looking at me. Good bye Shaun." she hung up the phone and cried as she made her way back to her room. Her heart was breaking and there was nothing that she could do about it. She had never loved anyone like this before and she felt that she would never love like this again.

CHAPTER 20

"Hello gentlemen." Rebecca said as they walked towards her in the terminal. "Thought you would never get here."

"It was all Kevin's fault. He was the one who was slow this morning."

"Everything ok?" Rebecca said to Kevin.

"Yeah, just a little nervous about this meeting. Wanted to make sure I had everything. Been here long?"

"Not really. I picked up some breakfast for us."

Kevin had a smile on his face. "Always thinking ahead."

"I figured the flight is a couple of hours, so by the time we get there, it will only give us about two hours before the meeting."

Black was already in the white bag.

"Girl, you sure know what a brotha needs," he said biting into his bacon, egg and grape jelly sandwich.

Rebecca always knew what each man liked for breakfast, hell it was her job to know. Black was just a country boy who always needed grape jelly on whatever breakfast sandwich he was eating.

She turned toward Kevin and replied coyly, "I like to think so."

She and Kevin shared a smile.

"Now boarding Flight 267 to Atlanta. First class passengers may now board."

"That's us dude and dudette."

"Come on slow poke," Rebecca said grabbing Kevin's hand.

"Whatever."

CHAPTER 21

Cheryl met Kevin about a year after graduating from high school. She had practically become a hermit in her room, never going out and never dating. By this time, her sister had two children and Cheryl loved her niece and nephew like nothing else in the world. Angel dragged her out one evening on a blind date and the guy seemed just as unimpressed with her as she was with him.

"Just come on, it will be fun." Angel said to Cheryl as she pulled her up from the bed.

"I don't want to go besides he is you friend, not mine. He probably is ugly anyway." she said with a smile.

Angel pushed Cheryl towards the bathroom and told her to hurry up since they would be there in less than an hour.

They arrived at the restaurant and Kevin didn't bother to acknowledge her at all until her Angel whispered something that made him smile. Cheryl thought that Kevin could probably have had anyone. He was a tall man with the looks of a model. He was a little conceited but she figured he had to be since he was trying to open his own business. Besides, weren't all men conceited when they belonged to a fraternity?

"So your sister tells me you broke up with your boyfriend."

Cheryl laughed to hide her nervousness and then simply answered yes."

"Guess you are on the market now, huh?" he said as he

picked up his soda and took a sip from the glass.

"I guess that's what you would call it."

"So, what kind of guy do you like?" he said.

Cheryl thought she noticed him roll his eyes to the top of his head a few times but she was trying to enjoy the date. After explaining that she really didn't like the jock types but liked them more smart than cute, she got his attention.

"So you would date the brothers that no other women would." He said with a hearty laugh.

"I don't think that is funny. Besides my mother said that if you date a man that is cute, he will probably be a jerk or worse, gay. So I guess that means I couldn't date you." she said with a hint of a smile.

"Look, I aint all that cute and I don't think I like…"

Angel cleared her throat and pulled Cheryl's sweater and told her to go to the bathroom with her.

"I don't need to go." Cheryl said.

"I hear that girls can't use the bathroom by themselves, they always have to go two by two." Kevin said as he laughed so loud he shook the table.

Cheryl was fuming and couldn't wait to get up from the table, bumping it on purpose causing his glass of water to spill but he had quick hands and pulled the tablecloth up so it didn't get on him. She rolled her eyes as her sister pulled her away from the table.

They walked into the ladies room and Angel was all over her.

"What are you doing, good lord; you are going to make him leave."

"Good, I don't like him anyway."

"Girl, you better get a grip. I am trying to help you out and you are being rude." Angel said as she applied another layer of lip gloss to her already shiny lips.

"Look, I was happy being at home. You dragged me out here with this jerk. God if he flexes his damn arms one more time, I am going to ask him if he has to do that to make sure they don't go flat."

"Look, just be nice and the date will be over soon. God, this is what I get for trying to help you out."

Cheryl went into the stall and said, "I don't need your help…wait…can you get me some tissue from the other stall…dang, I would pick the one without tissue in it."

Angel went into the next stall and pulled the tissue from the roll and tossed it over the wall to her sister.

"Thanks, and I promise to be nice when we go back out but I am getting tired and ready to go."

"Just another hour and then you can go back home and curl up in your damn den of loneliness."

Cheryl stepped out of the stall and washed her hands and looked at her sister in the mirror.

"Look, I'm sorry. Thanks for getting me out of the house. I do appreciate it but next time can I at least pick the guy."

"Deal." Her sister said as she held the door open for Cheryl.

Kevin and Cheryl started dating and immediately she saw things that she didn't like but her sister told her to stop being so picky or she would never find anyone. Cheryl didn't like the way he always seemed to talk down to her when they had a conversation and she didn't like the way he made her feel stupid if she knew the answer to things. The thing that stood out the most was that he never wanted her to have a 'real' opinion about anything. He wanted her to agree with whatever he said and if she didn't; well an argument would ensue and the night would be ruined.

Sure Kevin took her out to eat and unlike her previous boyfriends, they didn't go to any place that had a drive thru window. They were seated and after placing their order, there was the dreaded awkward silence.

"So what do you plan on doing now that you are officially an adult."

"Umm, I have always wanted to move to New York and become an executive assistant to someone famous."

"See that right there. You should always be ready to

answer a question like that."

"Well, you didn't let me finish."

"Well finish then." He said with annoyance in his voice.

"I would make that person's day flow effortlessly. Making sure that I had everything lined up so he/she could move throughout their day like a breath, without a thought."

"Oh, so I guess you do have some kind of sense." He said and looked behind him as the waitress walked to the next table.

Their food arrived and not another word was said until he paid for dinner and they headed out, only to be met by Brenda. She tried to keep it moving but she insisted on calling out Cheryl's name. Cheryl tried to grab Kevin by the hand but he didn't want any parts of it. Instead he went up to Brenda and started talking. When Brenda moved on he turned to Cheryl.

"Why were you so rude?"

"Whatever."

"Well, she told me that you used to date her man, but I guess that's in the past, since you are now my boo. Right?"

He slid his hand around her waist and pulled her in close for a kiss.

"So you wanna be my boo, huh?"

She didn't see what the harm could be even though her gut was telling her it was wrong but something in the way he had just kissed her made her feel special. She smiled and wrapped her arms around his waist and gave him a hug and told him that she would be his 'boo'.

Cheryl pushed herself up from the bed and limped into the bathroom. She turned on the water and as she applied the cocoa butter to the scratches on her arms she tried not to look into the mirror. She stepped into the shower and gingerly used the sponge to slide across her sore body. She let the hot water sooth her aches and pains and hoped that she didn't stiffen up when her muscles relaxed. She stepped from the shower, grabbing the thick brown towel from the rack and tried wrapping it around herself but when she brought her arm up and around her, the sharp pain sucked the breath from her. She decided to pat herself dry and then would use the baby oil and concealing powder. She walked back into her bedroom and sat at her vanity. As she leaned over to apply the concealing power, she noticed just how many bruises she had. The bruises were deep and many. They ran up her legs, arms and finally rested at her neck. She needed to apply more than she was used to but when she was satisfied she went in and woke up Donnell and Kayla for school.

"Donnell, wake up. After school I want you to catch the bus over to your grandparent's house."

"Why?"

"I just need a few days alone while your dad is out of town. Plus I want to do some cleaning and take care of some things."

"Or are you just waiting for the bruises to heal?" Donnell said as he swung his legs to the side of the bed. "Why can't you just tell us the truth?" he said as he stood at his full six foot height.

"Look Donnell, just do what I ask you to do without being such a smart-ass." Donnell brushed past her.

"Excuse you." she said as she caught him by the arm.

"Look, you told me, so get out of my room." he said as he yanked his arm from her grasp.

"I don't know who you think you are, but you better watch your tone!"

He continued to his bathroom and slammed the door.

"Look, you better get your ass together before you come out of there," she said as she turned and walked out of his room.

She walked down to Kayla's room and found her lying on the floor with her cell phone beside her "Sweetie, it's time to get up for school." Kayla stretched, rolled over and got up.

"Mommy, are you ok?" She asked.

"Yes sweetie. Why?"

"Cause I heard you and daddy fighting again."

Cheryl grabbed her and wrapped her arms around her daughter. "You know mommy loves you, right, and would never let anyone hurt you. Now go get dressed so you can have breakfast."

She walked into her bedroom wondering just how much Kayla had heard from the night before.

Donnell walked up behind her and caused her to jump,

"See if you weren't so scared of him, you wouldn't be jumping every time someone walked into a room."

"Donnell, don't."

"Mom, I just came to say I'm sorry. I didn't mean to yell at you earlier, but you have to stop letting him treat you like that. I get sick of hearing you saying you're sorry for him hitting you. It's getting a little old. But anyway, I just wanted to say, I love you." he wrapped his arms around his mother and Cheryl held back tears.

"I love you too; now go get ready for school," she said while pushing him towards the door, "hey, no matter what, make sure you always look out for your sister, ok?"

"You know I will," he said and walked back to his room.

She walked downstairs and made them breakfast. She yelled up to them.

"Come on you two, you are gonna be late." They came bouncing down the stairs with Donnell teasing Kayla.

"Look you two, come on, you act like you are two years old." Kayla kicked Donnell in the back of the leg while he tried to hit her arm.

"That's enough. Now sit down and eat. I didn't make this food for you all to play with it."

Donnell grabbed the syrup from Kayla's hand and the top fell off, causing half of the bottle to pour out on his plate. Kayla let out a loud laugh and Donnell threw the top at her, hitting her on her white shirt.

"Mom, he got syrup on my shirt!"

Cheryl got the towel and went to work on the shirt, "Now why would you do that?"

"Mom, she took the top of the syrup and now I can't eat

my food."

She looked at the plate full of syrup and smiled. "Next time, maybe you should let your sister use it first."

"See, I knew you were going to say that. That's why she going to school smelling like a waffle house." This time it was Donnell's turn to let out a loud laugh.

"Look, grab another small plate and put another pancake on it and get some of that syrup and let's go. You are going to be late." She said as she tossed the towel on the counter.

As they grabbed their lunches, she followed behind them and felt a twinge of pain in her chest. She brushed back the tear and got into the car. She backed out of the driveway and saw Donnell hooking up his IPod to the rear seat.

"Mom, I left my IPod in the house." Kayla said.

"Sorry, we are already late."

"But I don't have any music to listen to." She whined.

"I have the radio on."

"You aren't listening to what I want to listen to. I had already downloaded all my songs for today."

"Well, I guess you will hear them tonight."

"Here," Donnell said, "plug in and listen with me." He handed her the extra set of earplugs and they were off into their own little musical world for the next fifteen minutes.

Cheryl pulled in front of the school and had just turned around when Kayla jumped from the truck before it stopped moving.

"Bye ma!" she shouted as she was already moving towards the front of the school. Donnell took his time getting his books.

"Ma, promise me that no matter what, you won't let him do this anymore. I can't stand to see you trying to cover up bruises all the time. Besides you are not doing a very good job and I hope you fix that before going anywhere else," He said while touching the side of his mother's neck.

"Have a good day honey," she said while he got out and

leaned into the open window.

"You too ma," he said and blew a kiss.

He caught up with Kayla and slapped the back of her neck as he passed her. She tried hitting him back, but he was too fast so she turned and waved before Cheryl pulled away from the curb. She smiled inwardly.

She set out to do her daily errands before she had to pick them up from school. She picked up some groceries and a couple bottles of wine. She went to the dry cleaners to drop off Kevin's suits and instinctively stuck her hand in the pockets and came out with two unused condoms. She dropped them in her purse without a second thought. Before she knew it, it was time to pick them up from school. Kayla was all excited about some trip that the step teams would be taking in the spring and Donnell was talking about shooting basketball with his friends at his grandparents' house. She arrived at her parents' house. After the usual greetings her mother pulled her to the side.

"What is that?" she asked Cheryl when the kids went in to talk to their grandfather. She was pointing at one of the more obvious bruises.

"Ma, you know how men can get in the heat of the moment."

"Ok, child," she said with a wave of her hand. "I don't need all of the details."

Kayla quickly chimed in, "They were fighting again," and walked back into her grandfather's room.

Cheryl's mom raised her eyebrows and said, "You aren't nagging that poor boy again are you? I thought he was going out of town."

"How do you know that?"

"He called me a little earlier when he couldn't reach you on your cell and told me to tell you to call him."

"Oh did he now?" she said as she continued to walk towards her parents' bedroom. She flopped down on the bed as her mother came in behind her and pulled her feet from the bed and swung them back towards the floor.

"Keep your feet off my bed." She said as she walked

over and sat down on the right side of the bed.

"Thanks for letting the kids stay here for a couple of days. Here is some money in case they want to order out or something. I'll pick them up on Sunday." Her mom took the money and put it on the dresser.

"You know you don't have to leave that money here. Your father and I love having our grandbabies here."

"Lord, don't let them hear you call them that. They think I baby them enough as it stands."

She kissed her mother on the cheek and headed into her dad's bedroom. He was sitting there beating Kayla in a game of spades.

She sat down and gave Kayla a hug from behind.

"Are you coming back?" Her father asked her. "You know you barely come over anymore. I miss talking to my favorite girl."

"Don't be telling that girl that, that is exactly why she gives Kevin such a hard time," Her mother yelled from her bedroom.

"What are you talking about? Ain't nobody said nothing about giving him a hard time."

"Never mind," her mother yelled.

Just like that an argument had started between her parents. She had gotten used to the petty arguing when she was younger, now it was just comical.

"You know your granddad cheats." She told Kayla as she got up and kissed the top of her daughter's head.

"Granddad, you wouldn't cheat would you." Kayla whined with a smile.

"Now why you go and tell that child that. Ain't nobody cheating but if she ain't paying attention; well that's her own fault." He said as he grabbed the other king from the pile of cards on the bed.

Chapter 22

"Hey Kev. You have got to come out and meet her. You are going to be pleasantly surprised."

Kevin walked into the outer office and was surprised.

He had heard how nice on the eyes this woman was but she was really nice on the eyes.

"Miss Hardy?" Kevin said while extending his hand.

"Yes." She looked up and into his eyes.

Kevin was speechless. Her beauty took his breath away. She was truly a breath of fresh air and that smile of hers could melt all the ice in Alaska.

"Kevin Goldman, how are you?" he said.

As she took his hand she looked him square in the eye.

He was immediately impressed that this woman was not afraid to look a man in the eye and hold the stare.

"I'll let you finish up here and Ashley will show you around a bit. Then you can join Mr. Marbury and I in my office. Kevin walked back into his office.

"Well?" Black said.

"Man, she is hot." Kevin answered.

"And the brotha is back." Cory teased.

Kevin was working on his latest proposal for one of their clients and having trouble retrieving the file from the database. Rebecca had come in to offer her assistance. As she bent down to help him they stared into each other's eyes. He whispered her name as his hands cupped her round ass and his tongue slid between the cleavage peeking out at him.

"Kevin, Kevin." She touched his arm. "I think I found the problem. It seems you have two files with the same filenames."

Kevin shook his head slightly to bring him back to reality.

"How stupid can I be?" he said.

"Don't worry about it. It has happened to me too."

As she got up and walked away, Kevin followed her.

When she reached the door, she turned and before his brain could stop him, he wrapped his arms around her and kissed her hard. She pulled away as if this had caught her by surprise and he felt his face flush with embarrassment.

"I am so sorry," he said.

What she did next surprised him. She stepped closer to him and wrapped her arms around his neck and continued the kiss. When she broke from him she spoke before he could.

"Let me just say this: there is no need for you to be sorry. We are both adults and clearly we are attracted to each other. We have grown closer as friends. You have been there for me through my break up with Toni and I never thought I would become attracted to someone like you. So before you say something that you think you should, just know that I am fully aware of your marriage and of your commitment to it. "Whatever happens between us is between us."

Before she could say another word, he wrapped his arms around her waist and kissed her passionately. His hands explored her hips, her back, and her thighs and finally found her breasts. He raised her shirt and felt the soft material separating him from feeling her skin. He began to kiss her neck, and her breasts. Her hands were under his shirt, feeling his muscular arms and chest.

"Oh Kevin, I want to feel you inside me."

He lifted her leg and fell to his knees. He raised her skirt and began to lick her panties.

"Please Kevin. Take me."

His fingers slid inside of her and she let out a small moan.

"Oh yes Kevin." She could barely stand up.

He stood and lifted her into his arms and carried her to the mahogany desk across the room. He sat her down and swept the papers to the floor. Before he pushed her back onto the desk, she put her hand on his chest. Kevin spoke before she could.

"Ok, I want you too, but not here. Not like this. Doing it right here, right now, would feel good. Damn good, but if we were in a nice big comfortable bed, that would feel even better and make it even more special."

"Ok. You're right," she said as he moved away from her.

"Let me make a call."

"Sure. I'll be waiting." She said as she walked to the door.

He picked up the phone and made a few calls, including one to Cheryl, telling her that he would be late. He walked towards Cory's office but noticed the lights off signaling that he was already gone for the day.

Chapter 23

As Cheryl approached the building on the left, she began to rethink her decision to be there. Her thoughts were all over the place. Was she doing the right thing? Maybe she should just talk to Kevin and give him a choice of staying married or going to be with whoever was taking up most of his time.

She wiped her eyes, put on some makeup and found the suite number. She walked in and saw women of all ages sitting there. Her resolve was falling because seeing these women was like looking in a mirror. Her husband didn't beat on her on a regular basis and he only did it when she pushed him too far. She turned to leave but as she reached for the doorknob, the clerk came over.

"Can I help you?"

"I am sorry, I shouldn't be here." She said as she turned the knob and opened the door.

"That is what a lot of women think," the mild-mannered woman said. "Why don't you come on back and calm down for a moment, then let's see if you still need to talk to me, ok?"

The woman guided her away from the door and led her down the small hallway. They reached the spacious room and the woman gave her a bottle of water and allowed Cheryl to sit down in one of the oversized chairs.

Chery felt as if she needed to explain. "We start arguing and then he loses control of himself and he pushed me and well…I should go."

The mild mannered woman never stepped away from Cheryl. She kneeled down in front of her and placed her hand on Cheryl's knee. She spoke softly.

"Ma'am for all the times I have heard that most women say it after their husband or boyfriends hit them, it's always the same. And trust me; if it happens once, it will happen again."

"I won't let it."

"How can you be so sure?"

"Because I am not like any of these women. I have …" Cheryl started to say but the woman cut her off.

"Let me interrupt you. Most of these women have college degrees, and live in million dollar homes, and have decent jobs. Now tell me what you were about to say."

Cheryl felt her face flush and she stumbled over her words, "Cause I won't let it happen again. I will call the police."

"Did you call them this time?"

"No."

"Why?"

"Because they would have arrested me, this time. This time I hit him first."

"So that gave him the right to choke you?"

"No, but I provoked him. Look I'm sorry for taking up your time. I promise you will not be seeing me again."

Cheryl stood and the woman stood also. She backed away and gave Cheryl room to move.

"I sure hope not," the woman said as Cheryl started to walk away.

"What is that supposed to mean?"

"I hope I don't see you anymore, least not on the news for a totally different reason, but please feel free to call or come back if you ever need to talk."

She reached onto the counter and pulled one of the business cards from the holder. She placed it in Cheryl's hand and watched as she walked out the door.

As Cheryl walked outside, the reality of her situation hit

her and she drove to the only person that would know how she was feeling.

Her best friend Dee.

She stood on Dee's doorstep and wondered how she would explain it this time.

She rang the doorbell again. As she stood there, she tried to think of how to talk to her friend.

She pressed the button one more time, but after no one answered and putting the note on the outside of the mailbox, she drove home.

As she pulled up in front of her home, she noticed two huge bouquets of roses sitting outside her door. She bent down and carried them into the house and wanted to throw them in the trash. It was just another way that Kevin wanted to make her forget what he had done.

She noticed in that moment that her house didn't feel like a home anymore. She sat the flowers on the table inside the foyer and stared at the walls. There were no pictures of what she liked hanging on the wall. The only art work that hung there was what Kevin had placed there. She wasn't allowed to hang pictures of the African art that she liked because he didn't want his house feeling like "Mustafa lived there" as he always said. There were no shoes lying by the door, no half eaten sandwiches or dishes on the kitchen counter. No coffee cups in the sink or even a smell. Everyone's house has a smell. Dee's house smelled of vanilla or fresh flowers, depending on her mood.

Cheryl walked into her bedroom and was instantly disgusted. How many nights had he lain on top of her, wishing that he was with the other woman? Hell, she wanted him to be someone else too but she knew she would never have Denzel, or Tyrese, so her fantasies were just that. She walked back downstairs and looked at the flowers she brought in. she took the card from the pink roses and read the card.

I hope these flowers help your mood.

She grew angry.

How dare he? It was a 'mood' she was in? She guessed it couldn't be from him attacking her. No that would just be silly, wouldn't it?

She threw the card in the trash and snatched the card from the yellow roses. I hope you enjoy the beauty of these flowers, just as I enjoyed the beauty of your smile. Signed MTP.

It caused a smile to spread across her face. She stared at the card a little longer and moved the flowers to the island in the kitchen.

The phone started to ring and she answered it on the second ring, hoping it was Dee calling her.

"Hello?"

"Hello Cheryl?"

"Yes?"

"Hi, this is Matthew. I just wanted to check if you got the roses."

"Huh? Yeah, I did, but how did you get my number, should I be calling the police?" Her smile was long gone because now she wondered if this man was a stalker, a killer or worse, a rapist.

Matthew gave a little chuckle. "No, no, no. I simply called information. Your number is listed and I wanted to make sure you got home alright."

"Yep, getting home wasn't a problem."

"Was there a problem?"

"Not that you need to be concerned about."

"Why?"

"Look, thanks Matthew for the ride, and thank you for the roses, but you really shouldn't have. My husband will really ..." she stopped herself when she realized what she was about to say.

"What?"

"Nothing, thank you I must be going." She hung up quickly. She went back upstairs and took a shower, put on some shorts and decided to do some cleaning. She turned the ringers off on all of her phones and started the major cleaning that she felt needed to be done. She opened all of the windows and snatched down the curtains. She picked up the phone and called the junk man. It had taken more than three hours to fill six Rubbermaid containers with sheets, curtains, toys, shoes, clothes and dishes. The doorbell rang and she struggled to get the container down the steps. She sat the tub down by the door to make it easy for the junk guys to take away then opened the door.

"I was worried about you." Matthew said in a matter-of-fact tone.

"No need to be, you can leave."

"I will not. Not until you tell me what happened when you got home. Then maybe you want to explain what happened to your neck and legs."

She looked down and then hid herself behind the oak door.

"You really need to leave. The neighbors might see."

"And what if they do?" What will they do? Report me to your husband? Let me guess what would happen then."

"You need to get the hell away from my door and mind your business."

"Oh, I am minding my business. But if I leave, my first phone call will be to the police to tell them that someone is being assaulted at this address."

Cheryl noticed the woman with the small dog walking down the street. The dog began to bark as it came closer to her yard. The older woman looked much harder at them than she needed to, so Cheryl let him in.

"Good afternoon Mrs. Cochran."

"Afternoon, just walking Coco." The woman yanked the collar of the dog as she continued past.

Cheryl pulled the door open a bit more and he stepped in.

She stopped him, "You can stop there and, you have five minutes."

"Then you'll want to answer fast."

"What?" she asked him as if she didn't already know the question.

"Well, how did you "fall?""

"I didn't....well not that it's any of your business, but for your information, I went upstairs, forgot something and came back downstairs without turning on any lights. Tripped and fell."

He chuckled. "I have to give it to you, you are quick."

"What is that supposed to mean? First of all, I don't have to answer your questions and you know what, you can leave. You don't have the right to stand there and judge me." She snatched the door open again.

"You know, you are right. I have no right to judge a woman who is obviously happy being abused by someone."

"How dare you!" she shouted. "You have no right to stand there and talk to me that way. You have no idea what…"

He cut her off, "You are right. I apologize but I don't like to see someone being hurt. You are much too beautiful for that." His hand came up and touched her cheek.

She moved her head back and stood to the side.

"Look, you really need to go," she said in a shaky voice. She couldn't let her neighbors see a handsome man coming from her house. "Like I told you three minutes ago, I am not your concern. Besides I could call the cops and tell them you are stalking me. You sent flowers and then found my address and came here, uninvited and unannounced."

"And what would they say when they arrive and find me standing here, in your house."

"I would tell them you made me let you in, pretending to be someone else."

"Oh, you really are quick with the lies."

Opening the door wider, she said, "You really need to leave. I don't have to put up with this."

"And you don't have to put up with a man putting his hands on you either. Just answer me this, do you still have my card?"

"Why?"

"Answer the question."

"You are demanding, aren't you? But yes, I do still have it."

"Good, use it if you want to talk."

"I won't," she said as she slammed the door. "He had some damn nerve. What he needed to do was mind his own damn business!" she screamed to the walls in the foyer.

After the guy came and picked up the containers, she had gotten tired of the happy homemaker crap and decided to call her parents to check on the kids. Their answering machine came on after the third ring. Her parents probably had them in some restaurant by now. She called Dee and left her a message to call when she got home.

She felt her phone vibrate and answered without thinking.

"Look, I didn't mean to upset you. I am sorry for showing up at your house, but I was worried. I just wanted to make sure that you were ok."

"Look Matthew, I am a big girl. Now that you have eased your conscience and did your good deed for the day, I must be going." She slammed the phone down and walked into the kitchen. The phone began ringing again and she let the machine pick it up.

"Mrs. Goldman, I apologize if I upset you. That was not my intention. I was worried because such a beautiful woman should have nothing in her eyes but sunshine."

Who in the hell is this nut? I will definitely need to call the police if he keeps this up, she thought as she walked out of the kitchen and through the foyer on her way to the pantry.

She started cleaning out the kitchen cabinets, feeling like the maid of the house rather than the owner. After folding the last of the laundry, she flopped down on the bed trying to figure out what to do next.

Chapter 24

The way Rebecca had decorated her office was incredible. No wonder "Barbie" wanted to spend a lot of time in here. There were mirrors and a small fountain on her book shelf. The candles had the most sensual smell coming from them. Pictures of African American men and women adorned the walls. He wasn't sure if they were original works of art, but they were beautiful. He would definitely have to have her input to spruce up his bare walls. As he walked back into his office, he resigned himself that kissing her was a mistake, even though he felt so right about it at the time.

"Are you ready?" he heard a voice say behind him.

He turned around to see her standing there with a bottle of wine in her hand. The sensual way she looked at him was enough to want him to make love to her right there.

"Let's go."

Kevin pulled up to the Marriott hotel downtown. Rebecca had planned on staying in the car, but then he came around and opened her door.

"Should I be coming in with you?"

"Are you ashamed? We are grown people, doing grown up things."

Rebecca didn't bother to answer; instead she took his hand and so began their relationship.

Chapter 25

As he sat on the plane, with her beside him and Black on the other side, he realized that this juggling act couldn't go on forever. He knew what needed to be done and he planned on doing it on this trip. Someone wasn't going to be happy, but hell, he hadn't been happy for a long time either.

As they landed in Atlanta, Kevin's mind immediately turned to business.

"Black our meeting starts at seven; make sure you're there by six thirty, just in case they decide to be there early. This meeting will change the rest of our lives. If they agree to the terms of our contract, we will officially expand our business. We want them to know they are not dealing with amateurs."

"I gotcha man. I can feel the bar being raised. K & B are on the way. Move da fuck ova!"

He and Kevin gave each other dap. Kevin leaned closer to Rebecca.

"I would like you there tonight too. Things for you will be different after tonight."

"No problem," she answered.

"Tonight, the champagne will flow freely and the stars will be shining brighter." As Kevin, Rebecca and Cory recovered their luggage from the carousel, Kevin walked off to call Cheryl.

She had long ago given up the cleaning and was on her fourth glass of wine. Kevin had very good taste in liquor and always spared no expense. The trouble with that was, it didn't take much to get her buzzed. At least she was in a better mood than she was an hour ago. She stood, and began moving out of the library, but the room began moving and the floor seemed to be moving further away from her feet. She plopped back into the chaise in the living room, laid her head back down and closed her eyes.

The phone rang and woke her from her peaceful sleep.
"What?" she said into the phone.
"Cheryl?"
"What do you want?" she slurred.
"Why you sound like that?" Kevin asked her. "Are you ok?"
"Do you even care?"
"You sound as if you have been drinking."
"And what I if I have? Do you care? No. You don't care anything about me. Just enjoy yourself in Ohio or wherever you are and leave me the hell alone. I can't seem to do anything right anyway."
"Cheryl listen. I do care about you."
"Um-hmm"
"I do. You are the mother of my two kids. If I must say, you are raising them to be very good people. I don't like for you to talk like that. Promise me that you won't have anything else to drink, and for God's sake, don't leave the house in that condition."
"Unlike what everyone thinks about me, I can make decisions on my own and when and if I stop drinking this evening, it won't be because you told me to. Don't worry, the kid's won't see me like this, and I won't leave the house. I wouldn't want to tarnish your squeaky clean image. But what do you think your image would be if I call the police and tell them you left black and blue marks on

me and that you tried to rape me."

"Rape!" Kevin half whispered, half yelled.

She pushed on. "If the phone hadn't rung, you would have.'

"You are my wife," He said turning his back on his traveling companions.

"Yeah, wife, not sparring partner. Are you even aware that you left bruises, which I can't even hide?

"I sent you flowers and tried to apologize."

"Oh is that what that was. I thought that I was being blamed for you putting your goddamn hands on me. Then again, I thought it was because you wanted me to be reminded that I needed to be forgiven, or was it because I didn't call the police on your sorry ass?"

"Believe what the fuck you want, I only tried to say I'm sorry. If you stop stressing the hell out of me, I wouldn't have to do that."

"Yeah, whatever, tell that to the cops, better yet, tell it to the other bitch!"

"Look, I didn't call you for this; I called to see how you were."

"No, you called to ease your fucking conscience. I saw the condoms in your luggage. I guess I should be happy that you are using them, huh? I wonder how she would feel to know that you beat your wife."

"I don't beat you, I only hit you a couple of times, when needed. It was a mistake and you know it, so don't be getting all high and mighty. For all I know, you had been with someone else and then he didn't want to be bothered with your ass after he hit it and sent you home."

"Screw you Kevin!" she said before slamming the phone down. She threw the phone across the room and picked up the nearly empty bottle and drank the rest from it like a wino hanging out on the street corner.

Kevin hung up with a serious attitude. How dare she

accuse him of trying to rape her, she is his wife, not a stranger in the street.

He then thought to himself, "I did mean what I said, if I ever find out she has been with someone else, she would be sorry."

"Is everything alright?" Rebecca asked.

"Yeah," he snapped at her.

"Don't be giving me attitude; I wasn't the one on the phone with you."

Kevin pulled her closer to him. "I'm sorry. The phone call is nothing. Just something I need to take care of when I get back home."

He would definitely need to slow down Cheryl and her lunatic rants.

Kevin checked into his room with Black having the adjoining one. Rebecca's room was two doors down.

"Kev, I'm gonna shoot some hoops to unwind, wanna roll?"

"Nah, I'm gonna chill before the meeting. Gotta look ova some things anyway."

"Cool. Holla." As Black left, Kevin called Rebecca's room.

"And who is ringing my phone already?" Rebecca said coyly.

"Hey baby" Kevin said. "You settled in?"

"Yep"

"Up for a little company?"

"Always."

"Be right there." He said and placed the receiver back on the phone. He sprayed a little cologne and brushed his hair.

Rebecca answered the door with just her t-shirt on.

"Damn girl, you gonna make a man fall to his knees." "I hope so." Rebecca replied seductively.

As he walked in, her body pressed his against the door. His hands reached under her shirt. He cupped her breasts, lifting her t-shirt; he stood and stared at her beauty. His fingers traced a small circle around her nipples, and moved his fingers lightly across her skin. She was enjoying every second of this. He brought his mouth close to her breasts.

The sensation of his breath was driving her wild. His hand reached between her legs, and Rebecca tossed her head back. Her hands ran over his shoulders and he pushed his fingers inside of her; a moan escaped through her lips. She tried keeping her composure as he fell to his knees. His tongue joined his fingers and her wetness was unbelievable. He used his tongue to lick her clit, sending tremors up her spine.

"Oh, Kevin," she said, while he stood and met her mouth with his.

They inched closer to the bed and she lay down while Kevin kneeled in front of her and went back to work on her. Her back arched with every touch of his tongue and fingers. Kevin pushed her legs back to gain more access to her jewel. Rebecca groaned out in ecstasy. Her hands grabbed the bed covers. Kevin's fingers went deeper into her. Her breathing was becoming rapid and shallow. Her legs began to tremble and she was close to climaxing.

"Oh, Kevin. Oh baby." He worked his tongue faster and faster, while his fingers pushed deeper inside of her. Rebecca's back arched and her hands clung to the sheets. "Yes baby. Oh my…"

He came up to her and pressed his mouth against hers.

"Kevin, oh Kevin. I want you inside of me. Now. Please." Her words were choppy and almost a whisper.

Kevin's pants were around his ankles. His manhood was about to explode. Totally forgetting about the condoms, he reached down and pushed himself into her.

"Baby, please!" Rebecca pleaded.

"Oh Rebecca," he moaned.

"Harder baby," she demanded, and he obliged her. He pushed her legs further back.

"Oh yes Kevin, give it to me."

"You like this baby?"

"Oh yes."

"Oh Rebecca…" Kevin groaned.

"Give it to me baby!" Rebecca cried out.

"Oh Rebecca!" he said as his body convulsed against hers. "I love you!" Kevin cried out when he emptied himself into her. His breath was ragged as he rolled off of her and gathered her in his arms after their breathing returned to normal.

"We have to get ready." He said as he ran his hand down her arm.

Rebecca rolled away from him and walked to the dresser and pulled her brush from the overnight bag. Kevin rose from the bed and lumbered into the bathroom. He emerged ten minutes later as Rebecca walked him to the door.

He pulled her into his arms, "I love you Rebecca." He said as he kissed her gently on the forehead.

As a single tear fell from her eye, she whispered back, "I love you too, Kevin."

Chapter 26

Cheryl slept off the effects of the Linganore Sparkling Red Wine. She was definitely a little tipsy and on the verge of having a hangover. The phone was now on the floor beside the bed. She walked downstairs and made herself some toast. After getting back upstairs, she noticed her phone and the flashing number two.

She picked up her phone and dialed Dee's number as she started running water in the tub for a long hot soak.

"Hey girl." She said.

"Hey hussy, I got your note. Everything ok?" Dee answered.

"I guess."

"Why don't we hook up tomorrow for breakfast and some serious shopping?"

Cheryl felt the water running into the tub, "You don't have to work?"

"Duh, how many times I gotta tell you. Every other Friday is my day off. Remember?"

"Oh I forgot. Ok, sounds like a plan. I'll come over around ten."

"Ok, love you hussy." She said.

"Love you too." she sank into the hot water, and began to feel aroused. Dee's words came to mind.

Pleasure yourself. It beats being frustrated.

She moved her hand between her legs; feeling instantly embarrassed. She couldn't do it and instead lay back and let the warm water caress her into a nap. She was awakened by the iciness of the water and got out and sat on the edge of the tub. She slipped her feet into her purple slippers and slid the robe over her nakedness. The flashing number two was very insistent so she pushed the button to start the automated voice. She came to a message left by that familiar voice.

"Mrs. Goldman, please give me a call if you need to talk or just want to get out of the house. My number is 8042376245."

She listened to the message again and wrote down the number. She climbed back on the bed and laid across it. She closed her eyes and let the sounds of the wind lure her back into the land of sleep.

By the time she was fully awake and not part of her dream, the phone had stopped ringing. She was in no mood to talk to anyone right now so she turned back over and let the sleep fairies take her away.

She woke up about an hour later feeling adventurous. She decided to call him and let him know that she had gotten his message.

She was relieved when his machine picked up. She decided that it was a bad idea but she had to leave a message because she didn't want him calling her back.

"Uh, hi, this is Cheryl Goldman, I just wanted to call and apologize for my behavior earlier. Bye." She rolled out of the bed, and had to steady herself first.

"Wow, I'm still drunk?" she said as she had to sit back down for a couple of minutes while the room stopped spinning. She went downstairs and decided to call Kevin.

"Room 420 please." She waited for a while and was then transferred back to the front desk.

"There is no answer would you like to leave a message?" the man asked when he came on the line.

"Yes, hmm, just leave a message that Cheryl called?"

She hung up and decided she had tried to talk to her

husband but that wore her out and now she was ready for more sleep.

Kevin made it back to his room and noticed the red light was on.

"This is room 420, I have a message?"

The clerk told him of the three messages he had and wondered why she left her first name, instead of saying his wife. She must have been flirting with the front desk guy. He pushed the thought from his head. He didn't have time to think about her right now, he had way more important things to get ready for. With just under an hour before the meeting, he needed to make sure everything was in order.

Chapter 27

"May I speak with Cheryl?" the voice on the other end asked.

"Speaking."

"How are you?"

"Fine." Who in the hell is this? She wondered. "Look, if you're trying to sell me something, I am not interested." A hearty laugh came from the other end of the phone.

"Cheryl, I am not selling you anything. This is Matthew. I just listened to your message, and there is no need to apologize. I realize you were upset, no harm done. The reason I am calling you back is..." There was a pause before he continued "Well, you affected me so much in the past 24 hours. I have seen women go through some things, but you seem like a woman on the verge of falling off a cliff. There is a lot of pain and suffering all over your face. Please, don't shut yourself off from someone or anyone for that matter, who can help you."

"And you think you are this person." She was becoming irritated with him.

"Yes."

"Look, I am a big girl. I put myself in this situation, so I have to deal with it. It was a mistake letting you give me a ride home. It was a mistake accepting those beautiful roses and it was definitely a mistake inviting you into my home. You don't need to be concerned with my problems. Find someone else to help, because I don't need it."

"Cheryl, listen, it's not wrong to want help."

She jumped right back at him, "Look, the kind of help I need, no one can give me. No one knows the hell I go through every day. No one cares that I am not happy. Then you come along, like some black knight to save the day and you want me to believe that you, a total stranger, want to help me out for G.P. Give me a flipping break!" Her voice was breaking and before long the tears flowed down her face.

"So, you are blocking out help from everyone." He said.

"What the hell do you know?" she shouted.

"See, that's what I mean, as soon as you feel like someone is coming down on you, you put that fence back up again. Just now, you were opening up to me."

"I shouldn't have." She brushed the tears away hard.

"Yes, you should have." Matthew sighed.

"You really do need to stop. I guess you are used to getting women with those lines. It sure as hell won't work with me!"

"Why are you yelling? I am talking calmly to you. What lines are you talking about? I can see that you feel unwanted and unappreciated."

"Oh, so you are a psychologist now? You think you know everything, don't you? Well you don't."

Matthew interrupted her, "Then tell me."

"Tell you what?"

"Tell me everything." He said,

She ignored the constant beep alerting her to another call coming in and for the next hour she told a total stranger all about herself,

Kevin called Rebecca's room,

"Are you ready?"

"Almost. If a certain gentleman hadn't messed up my hair, I would have been ready twenty minutes ago."

"Mmm and how did he mess up your hair?"

"Well, he made love to me so good, that even my hair was too tired to hold a curl."

"He was that good?"

"Nope." Rebecca said coyly.

"No?" Kevin inquired.

"He was excellent."

Kevin whispered, "Well just wait until later, because it is on."

Chapter 28

Cheryl finally took a breath and wondered if Matthew was still on the phone,

"Hello?"

"I'm still here." He answered.

"I am sorry for subjecting you to my insane life."

"No apology necessary." Matthew said.

She glanced at the clock and at her phone when she heard that beep again.

"Oh my goodness, I must let you go. It's getting late and I have to call him back." She said standing in her room looking around.

"Look, before you hang up, you have my number and I don't want you to be afraid to use it. One more thing, I must tell you this, in case you haven't heard it lately; you are a very pretty woman."

"You sure could make a black woman blush. I am sure your wife is very lucky."

Matthew laughed at her, "very clever. However, I am not married. I've been divorced for two years."

"Oh, sorry. I didn't mean to pry. Why did she leave you?"

"You're funny." He said while laughing hard. "However, she didn't leave me, I left her. She couldn't handle it when I started my own company. There were times when she was the only one with money to cover bills. She couldn't accept that a new business doesn't start out making money. I struggled for about three years but then my break finally happened and when my business finally did recover, she wanted to be back in my life, which told me one thing. She was all about the money, so I asked for a divorce."

"Any kids." Now was her time to put him on the receiving end of the questions.

"Yes, one. A daughter. I hated leaving her, but a girl needs her mother, but I am a very involved father."

"Good for you. At least there are some men willing to be a father, unlike... Well, what business do you have?' "Well, the limo you came home in."

"Yes,"

"That's my business."

"Oh, you must be doing very well, because that limo was very nice."

"I am doing ok. Right now we have ten stretch limousines, two Navigator limos, one Escalade limo and soon to arrive three Hummer limos."

"Wow, I am impressed. Congrats on the new vehicles."

"I would love to take you out in the Hummer limo when they come in."

"Thanks, but I don't think so. My husband wouldn't approve."

"Well, your husband doesn't have to approve. Its ok for you to have a friend isn't it?"

"Female yes, males no."

"We shall see." Matthew replied.

"I must be going. Thanks for listening to me."

"Hey, I am going to grab some dinner, would you like to come along."

"No thank you. I really can't."

"Why, got other plans with your husband?"

"No, no plans. He isn't home anyway."

"Great." Matthew said a little too quickly. "Since I already know where you live, the limo will be there in an hour. Dress casual. See you in an hour."

"But-."

Her objection wasn't heard because the phone was

already dead. She dialed Dee's number.

"Hey."

"Hey yourself."

"Guess what."

"Now you know I hate guessing game." Dee said.

"Ok, what would you say if I say I met a guy?"

"That you were lying."

"Well, I'm not lying. He is so nice. He listened to me for over an hour, ranting and raving about Kevin."

"Whoa. Get up" she said to whomever she was with. "You told this dude about your husband."

"Well, kind of. He already knows him."

"Ok."

"Not like that. Something happened last night and this guy came to my rescue."

"Rescue?"

"Never mind all of that. Anyway, he let me use his limo to get home and then he sent me roses and then came by the house."

"Beep. Beep. Beep. Back up the turnip truck. You let this guy come to your house. Girl, do you know what will happen if Kevin finds out?"

"What Kevin don't know, won't hurt him."

"No, but it will hurt you. You better be careful girl."

"I will. I'll tell you about it tomorrow."

"Tell me what tomorrow?"

"About dinner."

"Dinner? What in the hell?" Dee shouted.

"Look, enjoy the rest of your evening. I'll tell you all about it."

She hung up the phone and ran to the closet like a woman going on her first date. She threw on some jeans and a tight sweater. After rethinking the sweater, she pulled on a blouse and blazer. She pulled her shoes from the closet and walked by the window when she saw the limo arrive, exactly an hour later. She went downstairs, pulled the front door open, doubled back to set the alarm and walked out of the house with the neighbors all preening their necks to see what was going on. She smiled and waved as she continued to the car, pulling her glasses onto her eyes as she did. The driver got out and held the door for her as she climbed in. Matthew was sitting there; looking very different from when she had seen him before. His bald head was so smooth it looked like a bowling ball.

"Hello again." He said in a seductive voice, while giving her a hug.

"Hello." She said as she climbed in and noticed the bouquet of yellow roses on the opposite seat.

"Those are for you."

"Thank you, but this was not necessary." She said as she picked them up and put them to her nose.

"I know...I wanted to."

"Well, thank you." As they drove along, he poured her some wine.

She held her hand up, "No, thank you. I had enough earlier."

"Would you like a soda or something?"

"Thanks a soda would be nice."

He opened the small compartment on the side and fished out a small can of soda. He opened it and handed her a napkin along with the can.

"You look really nice...damn." He whispered.

"Excuse me?" she said looking up from her drink.

"Oh, nothing."

Kevin tried calling the house one more time. Shit. Where was she? He even tried her cell but her voice mail came on immediately. She sure knows how to piss me the fuck off. This is why he had decided that he needed to be free of her dead weight. He was tired of going home to her. If he could divorce her this instance, he would; that way he could be the woman he really wanted. He went to Rebecca's room and they rode down to the meeting together.

They walked into the downstairs restaurant and saw the four men sitting together deep into conversation.

Kevin spoke first and introduced Corey and Rebecca. They sat down and immediately got involved in the conversation of letting them become affiliates of their public relations firm.

"So what do you think the name of this establishment should be?" Corey asked as the men continued to talk about the location.

William spoke up, "We were thinking to use our last initials, H, E and W….and say an affiliate of K & B.

"Of course that would need to be on all of the signage that you had made." Kevin said.

"Naturally." Edward said.

"As long as you know that you aren't entitled to anything but the affiliation tag," Howard said.

"I don't expect anything except for your check to clear and our monthly meetings like we discussed."

"That sounds like we have a deal." Corey said

"Not so fast. We need to look over the paperwork and then let you know."

After another round of drinks for everyone, Howard, Edward and Williams excused themselves and told Kevin that he would have an answer for them by eight o'clock the next morning.

The meeting was over and Kevin was nervous.

"How do y'all think the meeting went?" He asked them while they walked to the bar.

"Man, why you sweating. You ain't got nuttin to worry about. They want in, and they want in bad. They were trying to be cool, but did you see their eyes when Rebecca gave them the numbers for the past three years?"

The excitement was contagious. Rebecca, Black, and Kevin were all smiles, when Kevin's cell phone started ringing. He excused himself and walked towards the bank of elevators. He pressed the up arrow and his face was tight. As he stepped off the elevator, he dialed Cheryl's number again. She had some fucking nerve, calling her parents and getting them all worried. Telling them she was going out to dinner and they could hear she was drunk, and now no one has heard from her. He dialed Dee's number.

"Where your girl at?" He demanded into the phone.

"How should I know?" She answered.

"Look, she tells your ass every fucking thing."

"Look, you might talk to her that way, but I ain't your damn wife." The sound he heard next was the dial tone.

"Fuck!" he shouted, as he approached his room, causing another couple in the hallway to turn around. He was so angry he couldn't get his keycard to work in his door. By the time he finally got into his room, he threw a glass against the wall. He dialed her phone again and this time she answered.

"Where the fuck are you?" he screamed into the phone.

"Dinner."

"So you couldn't call anybody and let them know that? You got your poor mother worried sick about you."

"Why are you checking up on me?"

"I wasn't checking up on you, I wanted to see what the kids were up to. When you didn't answer your phone, I called your mom who told me that you dropped them off."

Cheryl answered, "I told them I would be out, and if they needed me to call me on my cell."

"Is this thing on? Did you hear me say I was calling you and so were they?"

"Well, I didn't hear my phone."

"Well, they have been, just like I have, and your fucking ass wasn't picking up. Didn't I tell you not to go out in public drunk?"

"You are such a piece of work Kevin. I swear. I am a big girl and if I choose to have some fucking wine, I don't need to call you nor my parents to ask permission. Besides, if it was an emergency, I would have called them back."

"Don't give me no fucking attitude. I can't deal with your ass here so you better watch yourself. You better not be driving."

"No, I am not driving."

"So how the fuck did you get out?" he demanded.

"Why do you care, remember; you aren't here. Oh, let me guess your little girlfriend not there with you? Hmm?"

"Don't get cute! I ain't in the mood for your bullshit!"

"I am not in the mood either."

"I'll deal with this when I get ..." he started to say but the phone was already dead.

"Is everything ok?" Matthew asked.

"Fine, but I've lost my appetite. Can we go?" She asked while pushing her chair back and standing.

"If that is what you want." He said and motioned for the waiter. He laid some money on the table and guided her back through the restaurant.

The limo was waiting for them at the curb. She got in and he got in beside her.

As they rode, she turned and smiled at him. She leaned over and kissed him.

"I'm sorry, I really shouldn't have done that. Can you take me home?" she moved to the seat across from him.

"Are you sure?"

"Yes."

They rode in silence. The car stopped and she didn't wait for the driver to get to the door, she was out and walking towards her front door with her keys in her hand.

"You forgot these." He said as he came up behind her and handed her the roses.

"Thank you." She said as she took them and unlocked the door.

"I had a nice time tonight. Maybe next time we will actually get food." He smiled and kissed her on the cheek and turned and walked back towards the limo. She leaned against the door.

She smiled back and held the flowers to her nose. She unlocked her door and watched as he walked away. She turned on the lights and saw the first dozen roses sitting there. She put the second bunch of roses in the vase that used to have Kevin's in it. She carried them upstairs and saw that there were some messages.

"Message one"

"Girl, Kevin just called and is freaking out. Call me when you get this."

"Message two: you better call me as soon as you get in the house."

She pressed the number seven.

"Message Deleted."

"Next Message."

"Cheryl, it's your mother, we are concerned about you. Have you been drinking?"

"Message four: Cheryl, where are you? This is your husband. You better call me when you get this message."

She pressed number seven.

"Message deleted, next message."

Again she pressed number seven

"Cheryl I had a nice time. I love the way you smile, don't ever let someone take that. Have a nice night."

She pressed the number seven but not before listening to it again.

She called her mom first and had to listen to the lecture about the dangers of drinking and driving and told her a lie that Kevin was on the other end so she could get her off of the phone. She hung up from her and called Dee who had millions of questions that she dodged or just didn't answer.

"Now that the world is taken care of, I can make that last call." She said as she dialed the hotel

"What did you want?" she asked as soon as he picked up the phone

"Are you home?" he asked her in return.

"I'm calling on the house phone aren't I?" she said.

"I'm the one who should be asking the fucking questions here!" he yelled.

"Well, anyway, I was just calling you back since I HAD to call you when I got in."

"I told you go have some fun, not go out and get fucking

drunk. You are such an embarrassment that I don't know what to do with you."

"You don't have to do a thing with me." She shot back.

"Oh, you have a smart mouth when I'm not around. Well let's see if you have that same mouth when I get back?"

"Whatever. Is this what you wanted?" she asked.

"Don't get cute." He shouted back "You acting all shady and shit and now you call me with fucking attitude."

"Whatever. I'm tired of talking. I am ready for bed."

"I don't give a fuck if you are tired, you gonna listen to what the fuck I have to say! I bust my ass for you and you don't appreciate shit."

"Whatever, did you and my mom come up with that line? I have busted my ass for you and this marriage and I get kicked in the teeth for it. I guess the girlfriend is the only one who understands you, huh?"

"Let me tell you one fucking thing, she is twice the woman you will ever be. She appreciates the small shit I do for her and don't complain either. I was going to wait until I came back to tell you this, but I want a divorce and I am moving out as soon as I get back!"

"What…what…wait." She stammered into the phone. "Kevin, you don't mean that. You would never leave me would you? I mean, I know we have our problems. We can work this out, I know we can."

"So now you aren't so tired, are you? Bitch you are a piece of work you know that?"

"I'm just tired, that's all. It has been a long day and…"

"Shut the hell up! Now you want to fucking explain. You better be glad I'm not there. Just remember what I said, this marriage is over. I need a real woman and you are not it!"

She stood in the middle of her bedroom. She heard the annoying sound coming from the phone but she couldn't grasp what had just happened. She had to make this right, somehow.

Kevin slammed the phone down and let the curse words fly. He had just about enough of her smart mouth and as soon as he got home he would deal with that. Then he would make sure his daughter was taken care of and then leave her.

He called Cory and told him he would be turning in for the evening. He had a lot of thinking to do.

He decided to get the ball rolling on one of his plans. He called Rebecca to his room.

Rebecca arrived and his eyes couldn't help but stare at how pretty she was. She was everything that Cheryl was not.

"What's wrong?" she asked.

"Uh, Cheryl and I just had a big blowup and I told her I wanted a divorce."

"Whoa. Are things that bad?"

"Not only are they that bad but sometimes she pushes me so far that I forgot myself and I do things I don't want to."

"Like what, things exactly have you done?" she said as she sat down in the chair facing the bed.

He sat in the chair at the desk and leaned forward, with his elbows resting on his thighs and his head in his hands.

"Look, I've done some things while I have been married to her that I am not proud of but I don't..." he stopped and looked at her when she grabbed his hands.

"Well, you brought it up. I am only trying to help or listen or be whatever you need me to be right now. You look like you have a lot on your mind. I just want to ease some of that. Today was a great day and I don't want anything spoiling it." She said as she pulled his hands down from his face.

"I'm not proud but sometimes Cheryl pushes me to the point that I grab her and have to shake her a little; you know, nothing hard or anything, but you know just hard enough to make her stop talking. She has this habit of nagging and it gets on my nerves."

She pulled herself up with his hands and hugged him tightly. "Tell me what you want. I will be there for you, no matter what. Ok. A man in your position shouldn't have to worry about his wife stressing him out and not being in his corner. Please know that I am always in your corner."

He hugged her tightly; breathing in the smell of her shampoo and letting the feeling of security wash over him like a hot shower.

"Thank you." He said into her shoulder, "I knew I could count on you."

"Now, tomorrow when we sign that contract that will be a big day for us. So I think we need to get some rest." She said as she pulled away from him.

"You want to stay here tonight?"

"Now you know I want to but what is our rule?"

"Hey I know. When it is time for business it's time for business."

"Exactly, I will say this; tomorrow night, we will have our own celebration. Deal?" She kissed the side of his neck and let her teeth nip at his ear.

He let her go after a prolonged kiss and made another call to his lawyer. He wasn't sure of many things but he was sure that he wanted her to be a partner along with Corey He knew Corey wouldn't go along with his idea, but he would need to deal with Corey's reaction tomorrow. Right now he wasn't going to let anyone or anything ruin his good mood.

Chapter 29

Things are going to change

Kevin had come home from his business trip flying higher than a kite. The business was expanding and the new investors were building an office in Atlanta. They deplaned and headed to baggage claim. Corey was already on his phone with Ashley and planning his evening with her. Kevin and Rebecca walked hand in hand to retrieve their bags.

As they neared the carousal, Kevin spotted his first and lifted it off.

"Rebecca," he said as he turned to her, "I know that this hasn't been the most romantic trip we could have taken but I want so much more with you." he said just as he turned back to pull her first bag from the carousal.

"This wasn't meant to be romantic. This was for us to push our company to another level."

"You're right but I wanted to spend some time alone with you, and I never get the chance to do that. I want you to know that I do love you…"

"I know." She interrupted.

Kevin rolled his eyes because that was the one thing that he hated about her. "Let me finish before you start being rude."

She smiled at him and let him finish.

"Like I was saying, I just want you to know that I do look at this like our company and I want you to feel that it is your company too."

"Not to interrupt you but my other bags just went around." She said as she pointed to the bags disappearing behind the wall and walked over to the furthest end of the carousel.

He followed her and as she pulled one of her bags from the belt, he grabbed the other.

She sat her bag down and wrapped her arms around him before she spoke.

"Honey, I know that you love me and whatever our lives hold, you know I will always be there with you. I took this ring to show you just how serious I am about you."

He hugged her tightly and let the moment take the stress from his shoulders. He knew at this moment that he wanted her to be a part of his everyday life. Kevin knew that Corey didn't like the idea and refused to talk about it in Atlanta. Kevin knew it would be a fight with Corey, who felt he was moving too fast but he wanted Rebecca to know he was serious so he presented her with a two carat pear shaped diamond, as his promise that in less than a year she would be picking out her engagement ring.

He came home and noticed the yellow roses on the counter. He didn't tell them two dozen.

"She don't deserve that much," he said to the air around him.

Cheryl wasn't home, but he could care less. He didn't feel like dealing with her bullshit just yet. Although he had just left Rebecca, he had to hear her voice. He went to his office and called her.

"Hey sexy."

"Hey yourself."

"Miss you.

"Miss you more."

"Love you."

"Love you more.

"You know, we can't have an entire conversation like this."

"Yes we can."

"I want to hear that sexy voice of yours."

"I can barely talk now. My throat is so dry. You can't keep doing this to me."

"I do not know what you are talking about."

"Really, having me beg and scream until the neighbors hear…I think you know exactly what I am talking about."

Yeah, but that is what turns me on. I can't get enough of you. It feels like I am going to explode.

"Well, each time you bring me to climax, it gets better and better."

"Yes, I noticed."

"Oh, did you now?"

"Yes I did." Kevin turned in his chair to see Cheryl's Expedition turning into the driveway. "Babe, I gotta run. I love you."

"I love you too." She said before hanging up.

He heard the familiar chirp of the kitchen door telling him that someone had just entered. He heard her footsteps in the kitchen and then walk through to the living room. He waited for her to make her way to his study but that never happened.

"Just as well; I am in too good of a mood to have to deal with her today." He said as he turned back in his leather office chair and pushed the silver button on the hard drive waiting for his computer to come alive.

The week progressed with cheerleading practice for Kayla, Donnell was at his friend's house and Cheryl wasn't talking. At least not directly to Kevin.

Kevin was in his office looking for files that he thought he had placed on the corner of his desk but couldn't find. He opened his office door and yelled up the steps.

"Cheryl, what did you do with my damn files that were in my office on my desk?"

"What files?" she shouted back.

"The ones that were sitting on my desk; the ones that were in the bright fucking orange folder."

"I don't know." She shouted back. "I didn't touch them."

Still shouting Kevin began walking up the stairs "You must have. I see you been in here cleaning, when I specifically ask you not to." He was now standing with her in the kitchen.

"I don't know how many times I have to tell you to let the damn cleaning service do it. At least they know how to leave shit alone."

She whirled around and slammed the towel on the counter, "well if you don't want me cleaning your office, say so. I swear I have to pick up after you like you are a teenager."

He grabbed her by the arm and she snatched away from him.

"What is your damn problem?" he asked her but she was already moving away from him.

"Nothing."

She moved into the living room and began pushing the vacuum around the floor.

He yanked the cord from the wall and she stepped on the pedal. She turned and saw him holding the end of the plug.

"I'm trying to clean." She said as she walked up to him and snatched the cord from his hand.

He grabbed her arm and spun her around.

"Kevin, what the hell do you want?"

"You better get ahold of yourself before I do it for you." He said as he let her arm go.

"Look, you have walked around here for damn near a week and haven't opened your mouth to me and the first time you do it is to ask about some damn files."

"You are the one walking around here with your fucking ass on your shoulders."

"And shouldn't I be. You call me from wherever and tell

me you want a divorce! What am I supposed to do? Jump for joy? Well, I will tell you this, don't push me too far Kevin or you will be on the losing end of it."

She turned to leave but Kevin grabbed her by the arm and spun her around.

"What the fuck is that supposed to mean?"

"Get your damn hands off of me." She said while taking a swipe at him.

"Don't you ever, in your small little life, threaten me, do you hear me?" he said and slapped her as hard as he could.

She slapped him back, more out of reflex than a purposeful act.

"Fuck you Kevin. I am not threatening you; I am merely saying the truth."

"Don't fuck with me Cheryl."

"Psst, if you only knew." She mumbled.

"What did you just say?" he said as he grabbed her by the throat.

"Nothing." She said as the act caught her by surprise and grabbed his hand.

"No, repeat what you just said little miss smart ass." His hands were getting tighter and tighter.

Kayla came to the door.

"Mom?"

Kevin loosened his grip and Cheryl started coughing.

"Yes sweetie." she said as she opened the door and rubbed the spot that Kevin had just released.

"See what you did" Kevin said while pushing past her.

"What I did? You the one acting all macho, grabbing all on me. You knew she was upstairs."

"I'm going out, and when I get back, you better believe we will finish this discussion."

"Whatever." she whispered.

After Kevin left she went into the living room and grabbed the cordless phone.

"Hey, can you talk."

"For you, anytime." Matthew said.

She considered Matthew to be a friend. He always listened when she called and needed an ear. She could talk to him openly about anything that bothered her and he always had encouraging words for her.

After she took a breath he again told her about leaving and how there were programs to help 'someone like her.' Although she knew he was right, she didn't want to subject Kevin to the humiliation of the bad publicity that would surround him if this ever got out.

Chapter 30

The wedding march.

Standing in the bridal shop, Cheryl was trying to forget what Kevin had said to her. Her mother wasn't helping the situation because she agreed with Kevin.

"Yep, even though Cheryl thinks she doesn't want kids, I want at least two. So I will do whatever is necessary to make that happen." He said while staring at her.

"You know sometimes that girl don't know what she wants. She can be a little flighty at times; you just have to know what to do."

Her mother continued pulling dresses and walking around with Kevin like it was their wedding and not her daughter's.

"Damn Cheryl, stop standing around looking lost. Go pick out something. I don't have all day to be in here shopping for your damn dress. I have to head to the Brooks Brothers to shop before it closes."

"Ain't nobody ask you to come anyway. Go on if you want." she said as she sucked her teeth and blew a heavy sigh.

He mumbled something and continued talking to her mother. The bridal consultant came over and finally took over the task of picking out some dresses for her to try on. Her dressing room was number twelve so she walked back while the consultant hung the dresses. She found a hand on her back and jumped.

"You startled me." she said when she saw that it was Kevin. "You aren't supposed to be in here."

He then grabbed her arm and tightened his grip

"Don't you ever speak to me that way in front of anybody. Do you understand me?" he said through clenched teeth.

"What are you doing, get your hands off of me." she said while snatching away from him.

"Look, don't make me hurt you. Make sure you know your place and make sure you don't ever disrespect me again. Do you understand me?" he said as he pulled her closer to his face. "And FYI, I don't like that dress. Pick something else," he said over his shoulder while leaving the dressing room.

Cheryl stood with her mouth open and a stunned look on her face. She swallowed hard when the door began to open. Her mother walked in, said something about Kevin not liking the dress and Cheryl told her what happened. The next reaction stunned her more.

"Well, sweetie, some men don't like to be embarrassed," her mother said as she walked out the door.

Cheryl took off the dress and tried on the others but they didn't give her the same feeling as the first dress. The one she really liked.

"I don't like it," he announced to the bridal consultant when she came out in another dress.

"Well, honey. It's not about you. It's about my bride and she really likes this dress. Don't you?" she said while turning towards Cheryl. She had positioned Cheryl on the small platform with the mirrors giving her the perfect angle to see herself.

"Yes, I think this is the dress." Cheryl announced.

He stormed from the bridal shop in a huff.

Two weeks before the wedding they were giving the caterer the final count of guests and confirming the limousines. The flowers had been ordered weeks ago, although none of Cheryl's favorites were going to be used. Kevin had decided, with her mother's agreement that since Cheryl was being a little extravagant with the catering, that the flower budget would be cut so they chose to use lilies and hydrangeas for the tables. Cheryl won the argument for roses for her bouquet after another week. Cheryl's father was telling her that she could have anything and even when Cheryl tried to take the cheaper route he insisted on her getting exactly what she wanted, much to the disgust of her mother.

Cheryl woke up the day of her wedding feeling very ill. She didn't know if it was about the wedding or about the wedding night. This would be her first experience being with a man and she didn't want to blow it. She wanted to talk to her sister but felt too embarrassed to bring it up.

"Ok, let's go. I have got to do something with your hair, since you didn't want to go the shop and get it done." her sister said as she bounced into Cheryl's bedroom.

"Ok, just let me wash it first."

"Girl, ain't no time for that. It is already eleven thirty and the wedding starts at one. If you wash it now, it won't be done before the wedding and Kevin said that you couldn't be late."

"Well, Kevin isn't the bride. Isn't the bride supposed to be late?" Cheryl laughed.

"Girl, just come on here. The rest of the girls are done. The photographer will be here in thirty minutes."

Her sister worked her magic and less than an hour later Cheryl had loose curls like a fifty's movie star. She started to cry.

"Didn't I tell you that there ain't no time for that? The wedding is going to be starting in less than forty-five minutes and you still need to get dressed and take pictures," her sister said while handing her tissues and pushing her towards the bathroom.

The wedding started about twenty minutes late, but everyone commented how beautiful it was.

Cheryl didn't eat at the reception because her stomach

was queasy. She instead settled for a glass of ginger ale and just a taste of cake. Kevin didn't seem to notice that she wasn't eating until the staff asked if she wanted a plate, which he promptly turned down. They danced their first dance and she began to feel more nervous as she could feel his manhood through his pants. There was no way around it, she was going to have to talk to her sister. She asked her sister to go to the bathroom with her. She made sure no one was in there when she blurted out,

"How do you know if it is going to hurt?"

"What?"

"You know…the first time…do you know if it will hurt?" she said as she sat down on the chair in the corner of the bathroom.

"Oh, it will, but you have to put in your mind, that you will enjoy it afterwards. Don't worry; Kevin knows exactly what to do," she said with a grin while fixing her lipstick in the mirror.

Around midnight the party was winding down so they decided to make their way to start their honeymoon. They got to the hotel and Cheryl immediately went to the bathroom to change into one of her bridal shower gifts.

"What is taking you so long?" he asked from behind the door.

"Just trying to unzip this damn dress."

He opened the door and turned her around.

"That's why I told you not to get this damn thing anyway," he said, while unzipping it.

"I'll be right out." She slipped into the red outfit that her sister gave her.

"What in the hell are you wearing?" he asked, getting up from the bed.

"Angel gave me this. I thought."

"I don't like it. Take it off," he said angrily as he finished his drink "Better yet. Come here."

She walked over to him and he grabbed her by the back of the neck and pulled her towards him and thrust his tongue into her mouth. The taste of the liquor he had finished was still fresh. He grabbed her around the waist and picked her up in one motion. He took her to the bed and snatched the fabric between her legs up causing the thin material to rip. His hands went up her stomach and to her breasts. He yanked his boxers down in one motion and used his feet to kick them off the bed. His penis pointed up to her covered jewel. His mouth came back to hers and he bit her lip causing her to yelp in pain. He pushed her leg to the side, and raised his body up. He looked into her eyes and suddenly rammed himself into her.

It took her by surprise, "Kevin. Wait. It hurts," she cried out as she tried to push him off of her.

"Oh God Kevin, wait, it hurts."

Again she tried pushing him off of her. Her mind was racing and the burning sensation was almost unbearable.

"Yeah, this is what you want. Isn't it?" he growled in her ear.

"No. No. Not like this. Please Kevin, you're hurting me," She said as she tried pushing him off.

"I told you I didn't like that dress before, but you wore it anyway," he said, still pushing deep into her.

The pain became so intense that tears were running down the side of her face. The headboard was hitting the wall with each thrust.

"Kevin, stop. It hurts. Stop it!" She screamed. His hand came down over her mouth while his other hand went against the headboard.

"Shut up, this is what you wanted, right? You wanted me to treat you like a common whore in the street."

"No, no, I didn't. I'm sorry. I'm sorry."

"Kevin moaned as he pushed harder into her.

"Open your legs," he demanded.

He took his hand away from her mouth long enough to pull her leg up to her chest and push deeper.

"Goddamn, you weren't lying. You are a virgin," he grunted. "Shit!" he moaned. "This is my pussy from now on. You hear me. Mine," he groaned into her ear.

Her groans of pain went unnoticed and soon the groans turned into sobs.

"Cheryl! Girl you are so tight, goddamn."

Kevin's body got rigid and then he fell over on her and rolled off her and began snoring. She eased herself from the bed and turned and looked at him. He was fast asleep. She didn't want to believe that this was how it was going to be. Nothing about her first time felt right. It didn't look like any of the movies she had watched. She walked slowly into the bathroom. She looked into the mirror and noticed the huge red spot on her neck. The spot Kevin had been sucking on. She felt something running down her leg and looked down and noticed the blood. She panicked. She walked into the bedroom and grabbed her cellphone. She dialed the only person she could think of.

"Angel," she said breathlessly. "I'm bleeding."

"So. You called me to tell me that," her sister said with attitude.

"I mean, from, you know."

"Girl, stop being a baby. That happens sometimes. Don't be acting new. Where is Kevin?"

"Asleep."

"Oh, you wore him out." She laughed.

"No, more like he wore himself out," she answered back.

"Look, get back to the fine man and don't call me no more." Just like that, she hung up. She opened the door to find Kevin on the phone.

"Yeah, send up housekeeping with some fresh sheets. Thanks." He had pulled the sheets off of the bed and then looked at Cheryl standing in the doorway.

"Oh, I'm not through with you yet," he said and walked into the bathroom.

That night lasted until late in the afternoon the next day. Kevin had sex with her over and over. When he finally stopped he turned her over and said, "Don't you ever wear something that I don't approve of anymore? Do you understand me?" She nodded and again headed towards the bathroom.

This time she ran a bath and eased herself down into it.

A tear streamed down Cheryl's face. The memory of that night was almost unbearable. She never would have imagined things could go from bad to worse. Her months of therapy told her that this was due in part to the feelings of worthlessness when her high school sweetheart left her for her enemy. Cheryl still loved Shaun and settled for the one person who gave her a little attention when she needed it the most. He showed a good side before he showed his evil side and sucked her into the fantasy world that she created in her mind. The only way to get out of this nightmare was to make a change and she was determined to do so, come hell or high water.

Chapter 31

"Where have you been?" Cheryl asked him.

"Out," he answered.

"With her?"

"No, at the gym."

"Don't lie. I can smell her cheap perfume."

"I don't know what you smell because I have been working out."

"I am sure you have," she answered back

"At the gym," he said.

"Yeah, right."

"I don't really care if you believe me or not."

"Not."

"Suit yourself. Any clean towels?" he asked as he began pulling off his workout clothes

"Hall closet," she answered him.

Kevin had the kind of body that made most women weak. His shoulders were well defined, his waist narrow but his thick muscular thighs were always prominent in whatever he wore. His arms were muscular but not overly. Women routinely commented on how sexy he was and he enjoyed the attention.

Cheryl tried not thinking of him in that sense anymore because of how bad things had gotten but something was pushing her towards the bathroom. She walked in as he finished brushing his teeth and knelt down in front of him and took his manhood into her mouth. He became aroused.

He grabbed her hair and moaned; "damn."

His hands were gripping her hair tighter as he continued to moan.

"Damn, that's right," he urged.

"Come up here," he said while standing her up. He bent her over the sink and drove himself deep into her.

"Oh yes Kevin," she cried out.

"Give it to me Cheryl," he answered. "Bang your ass into me." Their skin slapped together.

"Yeah, girl, give it to me." His hand met hers between her legs.

His hands cupped her breast and he began nipping at the back of her neck.

"Oh yes," she cried out again.

"Whose is it?" he asked

"Yours baby."

"Tell me again," he demanded.

"Yours," she responded.

"Ain't nobody getting this Right?" he said while pounding into her rougher. "That's right, give it to me. Give me my pussy. This is my pussy. You hear me!"

"Yes. Yes," she groaned out.

"I'm going to take what is mine," he said.

"Yes," was all she could mutter.

"Beg me Cheryl," he said while pulling her hair.

"Please, I want you to fuck me."

"No...I know what you really want!" Kevin suddenly withdrew, and pushed himself into a different target, a place he knew she didn't like.

"No" she cried out, as her hand left the sink and tried to push him out of her. "Aww."

Kevin. No. Stop," she cried out as her senses came back to her and the pain shot though her.

"You can take it," he growled and pushed her hand away. His hand grabbed around her throat and started squeezing.

"No," she whispered, while trying to catch her breath.

"Kevin, please stop."

"Oh Shit." He pounded into her harder. "Fuck!" he shouted as he let go deep inside of her ass.

He withdrew from her and quickly turned on the shower and stepped in. No words, no thanks, nothing.

Chapter 32

Kevin tried doing some work but his mind was elsewhere. He decided to give his boy a call.

"Man, Cheryl was acting like some whore I could pick up downtown."

"Sounds to me like she was trying to please her man."

"Please, any other time, she would be all offended and shit if I try going into the forbidden zone."

"Shit, if Ashley let me do that shit, I would give that girl the world. Hell I might even marry her ass."

"Nigga, you know you ain't getting married."

"That's right. You know my motto."

"Always a playa," they said in unison.

"Nigga, I gotta go, my other line is beeping. Holla."

Kevin disconnected from his call with Black and picked up the other line He didn't recognize the number but picked up anyway.

"May I speak with Mrs. Goldman?" The husky voice said.

"She isn't here."

"Can you let her know that…?"

"Yeah," Kevin said and hung up before the caller could say anymore. He had an attitude. Why is some man calling my wife, he thought to himself as the news channel suddenly came alive with a breaking story.

"An accident has shut down northbound 95 at the exit of Pennsylvania Avenue and Upper Marlboro. Both right lanes are closed so avoid that area if at all possible. There is no word yet on injuries."

After about ten minutes, the phone started to ring again. Kevin picked up the receiver and listened to the woman in astonishment.

"Where? I'm on my way. Kayla! Kayla! Get your shoes and leave a note for Donnell, your dumb ass mother has been in an accident," he said as he slammed the receiver down and put the glass on the counter.

Kayla started asking questions when she reached the kitchen.

"Look, just get your damn shoes and let's go!" Kevin got a shirt from the closet and pulled on his Jordan shoes.

He grabbed his keys and a bottle of water from the refrigerator and headed out the door. Kevin got into his Navigator and hit the On Star button.

"Cheryl's parents" he spoke.

"Dialing."

"Mom, hey, yeah, ah, Cheryl was in an accident and they have flown her to the hospital. Washington Hospital Center. Yeah, I'm on my way now."

He ended that call and again hit On Star.

"Dee."

"Dialing."

"Dee, Cheryl is heading to the hospital. What! Look! I don't have time for this shit; just get to Washington Hospital Center."

Another call.

"Black."

"Dialing."

"Black, meet me at Washington Hospital Center."

"Dad, is mom going to be okay?" Kayla said with her arms crossed.

"She better be," He answered her.

"Did you do it?" she asked.

"Do what?"

"Did you beat her up again?" She said while staring at

her dad.

"What? Look you better watch your tone with me young lady," Kevin said while looking at her and trying to maneuver around the traffic.

"Well, you didn't answer the question," She said and turned towards the window.

Kevin went to grab her arm and she snatched away from him and moved closer to the door. If the door wasn't closed, she would have surely fallen out of it.

Kayla and Kevin walked in through the emergency room entrance and went to the receiving desk.

"My wife was brought here." He said to the nurse.

"Name?" She asked without even looking up from the desk.

"Cheryl Goldman." She turned to the computer and typed.

"Come with me," she said, while standing.

As they were walking towards the back, her parents arrived with Mrs. Bookman looking annoyed.

"Is she alright? Where is she? What happened?" Mr. Bookman asked.

"I don't know anything yet, I just got here."

The nurse directed him to the back sitting area.

"Wait here. The doctor will be here shortly."

After a few minutes, a nurse approached.

"Mr. Goldman?"

"Yes."

"Come with me." The nurse took him to another part of the hospital. They finally came to a corner room and she told him to sit and wait.

"Look, you need to tell me something. I have been waiting for almost thirty minutes," he said with attitude.

"Sir, the doctor will be with you shortly," the nurse said with a little more attitude than he cared for. She closed the door as he was still asking for an explanation. Twenty more minutes had passed and finally the door opened and a doctor entered. Kevin rose.

"Have a seat." He said while pointing to the chair on the other side of the desk.

"After you tell me what the fuck is going on!"

The doctor sat down behind his desk.

"Yelling is not helping your wife, nor is being rude to the staff. Now, have a seat and I will explain a few things to you. Your wife is in critical but stable condition. She is unconscious but responsive. We are having a little problem stopping the bleeding that she has in her kidney. There is a small tear and she has a severe hematoma on her forehead and we want to keep..."

Kevin interrupted him, "Look, without going into all the medical jargon just tell me what the hell happened to my wife."

"In simple terms, it is hard to treat your wife because we first have to determine what she took. Does your wife do drugs, prescription or otherwise?"

"What in the hell are you asking me for?" Kevin shouted as he stood up from his chair.

"Again, there is no need for you to be rude," The doctor said.

"What? Are you kidding me? You are seriously asking me if my wife took some kind of illegal drugs," Kevin said.

"Yes," the doctor said while tenting his hands in front of his face.

"I think you better watch yourself doctor. That is none of your business!"

"Well, since you seem to be saying no, then there is only one thing I can conclude. I believe your wife tried to commit suicide. That is the only explanation. Your wife had morphine in her system. Now unless you tell me that she had back pain or some other surgery or ailment, there would be no reason for her to take that kind of medication."

Kevin sat down. "What the fuck?" he mumbled.

"Sir, are you ok?" The doctor said, coming to his side of the desk.

"Yeah," he mumbled. "This bitch…goddamnit. Look to answer your question, I don't know why she took morphine. I had some extra from an injury I had about a year ago. Look can she be arrested for this?" Kevin asked.

"Well, I can't say for certain. If you are telling me that you didn't know, then she has more problems than jail to be concerned about," The doctor said as he stood.

"Look I don't care about her other problems. I have a successful business and I don't need anything ruining my reputation in this city," Kevin said as he stood also and walked towards the door.

Kevin composed himself and walked back into the waiting room where Cheryl's family and Dee had gathered. He spoke calmly and a little above a whisper.

"Seems as if Cheryl has a little drug problem." He lied.

"Oh my God"

"Holy Shit."

"What. I knew that girl was weak but drugs?" Her mother said as she plopped down in the chair.

Kevin continued to speak. "She took some of my left over pain medication and then went out here and got herself into a car accident."

"What?" Why?" Someone asked.

"Why would she do that?" Mr. Bookman asked, looking at Kevin. "What did you do to her?"

"Yeah, Kevin; what exactly did you do to her," Dee demanded.

Kevin walked over and stood in front of Mr. Bookman. "I don't know why."

Dee spoke up, "Yes, you do. You made her do this Kevin. You asked that girl for a divorce, when she found out you were seeing some other woman behind her back!"

Kevin walked to her with his fists tight. Dee snapped to her feet.

"I wish the hell you would! I am not Cheryl. I'll kick your fucking ass!"

"What does she mean?" Mr. Bookman asked.

"Nothing for you to be concerned about, she is just

running her mouth as always."

"I am not! You hit her and you know it. She cries to me all the time, how miserable she is, how you don't love her, how she didn't know what to do."

The security guard walked up to them.

"Ma'am you will have to quiet down."

"Kevin, is what she said true?" Mr. Bookman asked.

"No sir. We have problems like anyone else and we argue, but nothing major. Look our concern needs to be Cheryl, not what some lonely woman with no friends has to say." He directed his comments towards Dee.

Mrs. Bookman came and hugged him. "It will be ok, she will be just fine."

The nurse came and said something to Kevin and while the nurse rushed towards the back, Kevin took his time.

He walked into her room and saw the tubes running from her face. The monitors were beeping in time with each other and there was a huge bump on her forehead that now looked purple and red.

"Make sure you do whatever you have to," Kevin said. He walked back out and saw all of the faces of her family and friends. He walked past them and straight out the doors.

Dee was on her way back in when she saw him leaving. She walked up to him.

"You lying son-of-a-bitch! You know damn well you are the cause of her being here. She couldn't stand to be near you any longer. She did what she thought she had to do. If she dies, it will be you that I blame."

Kevin grabbed her by the arm. "Keep your stupid thoughts to your damn self. No one cares what you think. You are supposed to be her friend, and here you are not even asking me if she is ok. You are nothing more than a two bit tramp, who doesn't want to see anyone happy. Cheryl's thoughts are screwed because of you, not me. Putting in her head all of that crazy shit!"

"I am her friend. You couldn't even have a conversation

with her unless you were putting her down, calling her names. You don't even know that I know what you called her. A rag-a-muffin, is the term I believed you used. So you just might want to take your goddamn hands off of me before I have your ass arrested!"

Kevin came back into the hospital and he along with the rest of the family waited for nearly four hours until the doctor finally came out.

"Cheryl is waking up now. She will be groggy but she should be fine."

The doctor pulled Kevin aside.

"We will need to address the suicide issue with her when she wakes up. I recommend that she seek treatment before she leaves."

"Thanks doctor, but I am not worried about that right now. I will think about that when she is fully awake." Kevin walked back to Kayla, Donnell and her parents.

Dee snuck in and sat beside Cheryl.

She began to talk, "Girl, I am here. Don't scare me like that no more. I am going to kick your butt when you wake up. Don't do this again boo; you know I am always here for you. I love you like my own sister, what would I do without you in my life? You know a lot of shit about me and who would keep me straight when I go crazy? You are such a hussy." She said through laughter and tears. "You just wanted someone to pamper you, didn't you? You know you can come home with me, just don't leave me Cheryl. You all I got girl. I know I'm being selfish, but please don't leave me. Girl, just get better, you got me in your corner. Don't worry, I'm not leaving."

Kevin walked in and told her to leave.

Mr. and Mrs. Bookman were just walking in as Dee said, "Well, I'm sure her family wants to visit with her too."

Mr. Bookman commented, "She looks so peaceful." He said as he stroked her forehead and kissed her softly.

Chapter 33

After five days, Cheryl was released and the kids had rearranged her room and pulled the covers on her bed back for her. Kevin was spending less and less time at home. He didn't bother to pretend anymore. The only time he went to their room was when he was drunk. When Cheryl first got home he was drunk and without asking, crawled into bed early one morning and had sex with her, then got up and walked out. Cheryl wondered if that was supposed to make her feel better, because it did just the opposite. She supposed the girlfriend must have been on her period or something. Why else would he even sleep with her?

A nurse that Kevin decided to hire came by every day to check on her and told him that her mood was declining. The nurse said she would have to let the doctor know. Nurse Vint came by one day and brought the doctor with her. Cheryl had been crying off and on for the past three days and the nurse was alarmed by it.

"Cheryl, what's wrong today?" he asked.

"I don't want to be here."

"Ok, where would you like to be?"

"Not here."

"Anywhere in particular you want to go?"

"Just not here. I can't even sleep anymore."

"When was the last time you had a good night's sleep?"

"About a week ago. I'm just tired." She said as she

rubbed her eyes.

"I bet you are. Would you like to have something to help you sleep?"

"Only if it makes me sleep forever."

"Forever?"

She didn't say another word. Instead she hung her head and stared at the bedcovers. She heard the doctor tell Kevin that she was suicidal and needed to get some help. She heard Kevin's voice. "What in the hell is wrong with her now?" he said as he stormed into the bedroom.

"There is no need to be hostile." The doctor said from behind him. "I think we should talk outside. They both walked back into the hallway. The door closed and the conversation continued to move away from her bedroom. Minutes had passed when suddenly the door flew open and Kevin approached her bed. Not waiting for someone to ask, he started talking.

"Look you need to get your ass together. This is some bullshit and you know it. I am not going to keep feeding into this shit, do you hear me?"

She began talking, to no one in particular, just talking; "I feel so lost. I feel so alone. I'm unhappy, and no one understands the pain I am in. It's like….like my soul is gone. My heart hurts and there is no sun or even the hope of sun. Everything is just so dark, I can't take it anymore."

She hung her head and cried.

The doctor came to her bedside and took her hand, "As you can see, she is extremely distraught. She is very suicidal and we need to get her to sign herself into the hospital."

Kevin got more attitude. "She doesn't need to be in any hospital. She needs to be home with her family."

The doctor pulled Kevin to him. "Mr. Goldman, you can see she is in no shape …."

Kevin cut him off and kneeled down beside her. "You hear them? They want you to sign yourself into a hospital. What about the kids, what about me? You don't really want to do that do you?"

She didn't look up. She let the tears continue to fall.

The doctor spoke up. "Cheryl we want you to get the help you need. You can come with me and talk to someone who will listen and hear what it is you need to say. Do you want to come with me and do that?"

She nodded her head yes.

"Cheryl, you have got to be kidding me." Kevin half-laughed. "You can rest right here and I'll send somebody over to listen to whatever it is you want to say. How can you even think about doing this to me?"

"Mr. Goldman, we will need for you to sign…"

"Like hell I will! All she needs is rest."

"What she needs is help. If you don't sign her in, she could very well succeed in taking her life the next time."

"Well then I guess if she does that it was meant to be, now aint it doc?"

The doctor pressed on, "Mr. Goldman, can you guarantee me that she won't?"

"Ask her yourself," he shouted. "Cheryl, you won't try this again will you? What about me and the kids?"

She shrugged her shoulders.

The doctor spoke up again. "We need your 100% guarantee that this won't happen again. Can you give us that? If not I can sign her in under an emergency hold for at least 72 hours."

Cheryl shrugged her shoulders again.

"I think it is in her best interest to be admitted." The doctor said.

"Cheryl, don't let them do this. I will get someone to take care of you."

She covered her face and cried harder.

"Look doctor, I need to speak to you," Kevin said as he yanked the door open and the doctor followed behind him.

"Who in the hell do you think you are! I know what is in her best interest, not you! How dare you tell my wife that she needs to be in some damn hospital?"

"I did no such thing," he said calmly.

"You have her believing she needs to be there. She needs to be home with her kids."

"Sir, she needs to be where she can't be a threat to herself."

"She won't be."

"Can you be so sure, she isn't?"

"That's because she is confused. She will be fine. I will hire someone to look after her."

"No offense, I am sure you mean well, but you are not equipped to handle…"

"What the fuck you trying to say?"

"Kevin is there a problem?" Unannounced, Cheryl's mom had arrived.

"Mrs. Bookman, they say she is a threat to herself and want to take her to the hospital."

"Oh, that won't be necessary. We can take care of her. Where is she, I will talk to her."

The doctor had a look of exasperation on his face.

"Of course we will need you to sign a release; releasing me from liability in case something was to happen."

"No problem, where are the papers?" Kevin asked. The doctor went to his car and came back with papers in his hand. He placed them on the table behind the sofa. Kevin went over and signed the papers while the doctor looked on. He picked up the phone and called the agency that he had hired right after Cheryl had the kids.

"Yes, I will need someone for at least a couple of weeks. My wife is recovering and I don't want to leave her alone. If they could be available 24 hours a day, that would be appreciated. Not a problem. Tonight if at all possible. Thank you." He hung up and called Rebecca. "I need to see you." He went upstairs and looked in on Cheryl; who was sleeping and Mrs. Bookman was in the chair looking at her.

"All she needs is some rest Kevin," she said.

"That ain't all she needs. I need to run out. Do you need anything?"

"No, take your time, I will be fine."

"Thanks mama, there is food in the fridge, and anything else you might need; well, you know where it is. I'll be back in a little while."

"Take your time."

Kevin walked downstairs and saw a brown Toyota stop in front of the house. The nurse was approaching the house.

"Mama, the nurse is here," He called upstairs before going out to meet her. He told her what he wanted her to do. They agreed on the payment and he told her that his mother-in-law was upstairs and he would be gone for a while.

He drove over to Rebecca's house and as soon as the door opened he began his tirade.

"How could she do this? Does she know how this makes me look? A man in my position?"

"Really Kevin?" she questioned.

"I am pretty sure everyone knows we sleep in separate bedrooms. Now her family knows I want a divorce. She is doing all of this so that I can't leave her ass. Don't you see? This is a plan of hers. How could I walk out on her now?"

"Let me ask you something Kevin. Do you love her?"

"No."

"Not even a little bit?"

"Fuck no! I love one person and that one person is standing in front of me. I want you to be my wife. That's why I gave you this ring. Now it seems like I can't leave her now, how would that look? "

Rebecca took a deep breath before she spoke, "I don't want you to do anything that makes you unhappy. I am here for you. I knew you were married when we first started our relationship three years ago. I know that you love me because of this ring. You need to do what is right to make her stronger and do what is right for everyone."

"See, this is exactly why I love you." He said while pulling her close.

"Baby I love you too," she said.

"Rebecca, I need you."

She pushed him back against the sofa and sat on his lap. She slowly unbuttoned his shirt and began to kiss and suck his nipples.

"Baby, you are making me hard," he moaned.

She continued the assault on his most sensitive area. She moved her hips slightly, just to feel his manhood grow harder.

"You want this Kevin?" she purred.

He could only nod his head; as words escaped him at the moment. She stood before him and while she pulled his pants down, she undressed in front of him. Her breasts fell from her lace bra, and she cupped them in her hands. He had his member in his hand. She turned around and bent down, stepping out of her panties. Her juices were running down her leg. He pulled her down on him.

"Ohhhh" she said as his hard penis entered her. "Let me do all the work" she said.

She rode him like a prized horse at the show. She worked her body slow then faster, faster then slower. He loved every minute of this. She threw her head back and he pushed himself into her further. His hands covered her breasts.

"Oh yes!" she screamed out.

"You like it rough, don't you."

"Yes!"

"You want it harder?"

"Mmm-hmmm."

"Tell me!"

"Yes Kevin. Fuck me harder! Fuck me baby!"

"That's right. You want all of this don't you?" He pushed his hips up into her. Her hips met his.

"Yes." He rose up and turned her over. "I want you from behind. Give it to me," He said while slapping her ass. He pushed back into her while grabbing her hair.

"Whose is it?"

"Yours!"

"Say my name!"

"It's yours Kevin!"

"Do you want more?"

"Yes!" she cried out. He withdrew from her quickly and plunged into the forbidden zone.

"Oh God Kevin! Yes! Yes!" The tightness of her made him explode.

"Shit. That was incredible" he said breathlessly. Sweat dripped from his forehead onto her back. He moved up to the sofa, but she wasn't finished with him yet. She lay on her back with her legs drawn up.

"Look at me baby," she crooned. With her legs open, she started to massage herself. As she continued to pleasure herself, he got down on the floor and his tongue joined her fingers. She grabbed his head and pressed him harder into her wetness. He pushed his fingers inside of her while gently biting her. He felt her muscles tighten against his fingers and pushed them in further. Her back arched and she cried out in ecstasy. He came slowly up her body and lay on top of her. After her breathing slowed to its normal pace, he looked at her. The unspoken words could be heard; loud and clear; between them and they fell asleep, spent and satisfied.

He awakened first, nudging her awake, he began pulling together his clothes.

"Do you have to go?" she asked as she rubbed her eyes.

"Baby, I don't want to, but…you know under the circumstances…"

She led him to the door and gave him a kiss and hug good night.

Chapter 34

What happens in the dark...

Rebecca's phone rang. "Hello," she said sensually.

"And hello to you too," the caller replied.

"What do you want?" Rebecca replied.

"Oh, why so cool. I thought you were happy to hear from me?"

"I thought you were someone else."

"Kevin maybe...nope but I miss you."

"How can you miss something that you threw away like yesterday's paper?"

"C'mon, don't be that way," the caller said.

"What way. Remember you forced me to leave you with your trifling ways."

"I know I made mistakes, but I know you still love me."

"Don't give me that. I have someone who really loves me, and only me."

"Oh does he now? How can that nigga say he loves you when he is still married?"

"That's none of your business," Rebecca said.

"Oh, did I strike a nerve? Calm down. Correct me if I'm wrong, but don't you go to bed alone every night and you wake up every morning, by yourself. From the way you answered the phone just now, you thought I was him. Probably sent him home with your scent and thought he was calling back. I know that voice, don't I?"

"Screw you!"

"That's what I want to do to you right now," the caller said.

Rebecca should have hung up the phone but instead she stayed on the phone and had phone sex with the woman that she should be over.

Kevin pulled into his driveway full of rage. After checking on her and telling the nurse what time she could report the next day, he went into his office.

He did a lot of shuffling that evening with his accounts and managed to open up two accounts for Donnell and Kayla. He wanted to make sure that his kids were taken care of, no matter what happened between him and Cheryl. He had also managed to sign three more companies to his agency and had at least three more on the horizon. The merger in Atlanta was well on the way to being finalized and the office was almost ready to be open. As he was closing the door to the office, the phone rang.

"Yes, this is her husband. What can I do for you? You can't be serious. What time? Ok. See you then."

He walked back towards his bar and poured himself a drink. He walked upstairs and saw her sleeping. His conversation with Rebecca instantly came to mind. Anger was starting to build the more he looked at her. You little bitch. He drank the last of his liquor and walked back downstairs. He picked up the phone and called Rebecca but she wasn't answering. He decided to check the computer to see if she was online, but she wasn't answering her IM either.

"Shit! Shit! Shit!"

He threw the glass against the wall. Kevin trudged back upstairs and into the guest room. He lay across the bed, but sleep was eluding him.

He must have finally dozed off, because the alarm woke him up. He walked into her room and looked down on her.

"The doctor wants us there by ten."

"What?"

"The doctor called. He wants to see you," He announced with attitude.

"Rebecca, will you just come on. Get up and get ready."

"My name is Cheryl," She said and got up and went into the bathroom. She threw up all of dinner from last night.

"Are you ready?" Kevin said, while knocking on the door.

She walked out and brushed past him. As she walked down the steps she felt as if she was about to topple over. The unmistakable feeling of nausea overcame her. Kevin caught hold of her arm as she swayed.

"Look, get it together. I don't want nobody thinking I threw your dumb ass down the steps," Kevin asked.

She yanked her arm away and continued down the stairs.

After riding for almost ten minutes, Kevin spoke up.

"We need to talk. Are you listening? The doctor said that your tests came back and he said one test came back positive. You're pregnant." He waited for a response.

"Did you hear me? I said you were pregnant."

"I'm not deaf, I heard you," She said as she swiped the tear away

"Well?"

"Well, what?"

"What do you have to say?"

"About?"

"Jesus Christ! Didn't you hear me! I said you are pregnant, as in going to have a baby."

"You don't have to yell, I am sitting right here. Don't worry, I'll make a decision."

"Decision about what?"

"Just don't worry yourself about it."

They arrived at the doctor's office ten minutes later and before the truck had hardly stopped she was out and going through the doors.

They waited in the waiting area for the doctor to speak with them. The wait wasn't that long, but to her it was like eternity.

"Good morning Cheryl. How are you?"

"Can we get this over with?" she asked the nurse.

"Sure, just let me get your chart and while I do that can you give me a urine sample?" He handed her the little cup and off she went. She came back and looked at him while handing him the cup and announced, "If I am pregnant, I do not wish to continue with the pregnancy."

"I'll let the doctor know you have something to talk to him about," The nurse said as he left the room.

Kevin bolted from his seat, "What the fu…I mean, what are you talking about?"

"Sit down and stop pretending," she said while staring at him.

Dr. Abalone walked in. "Good morning. Now, you know why you are…"

Cheryl cut him off. "I already know I don't want to keep this baby."

Dr. Abalone sat down and leaned back in his chair. "Let's calmly sit down and talk things through."

"I have already decided."

"I haven't," Kevin said.

"So what?" she yelled back.

"Mr. and Mrs. Goldman, I am sure this is a shock, but let's…"

"No, I don't want anything from him." She buried her head in her hands.

Dr. Abalone looked first at Kevin then back at her. "Let me speak with her," he told Kevin.

In a huff, Kevin left the room.

"Mrs. Goldman, why are you so upset?"

"You don't understand. I can't have this baby. I just can't. He doesn't even love me. Please just find me some place I can go to get rid of it. Please."

The doctor left her alone. Kevin burst into the room and grabbed her up from her seat.

"You can't do this!" he screamed.

"Get your hands off of me!"

Dr. Abalone walked in. "I will have to ask you to take your hands off of my patient."

"Look, I'm your husband and the father of this child."

"You're half right. You're the father of this child. You haven't been a husband for years. Don't even make me laugh with this show you are putting on for the doctor." She pulled away from him. "Dr. Abalone, I will call you tomorrow," she said as she walked out.

She turned, leaving Kevin standing in the office. He followed and when they walked through the waiting room, all the women looked up at him. As he caught up to her outside, he said, "How could you do that, you aren't considering it?"

"No."

"Look this is not a decision you make on the spur of the God dammed moment."

She kept walking, totally ignoring him and his curse words.

The ride home was quiet and heavy with tension. They walked into the house, her hurt and him fuming. She knew the entire time she was pregnant. The vomiting was the first clue and her cup size was another. She knew the day she tried committing suicide. A woman knows two things. One, when her husband is cheating on her and two, when she is pregnant. Sadly, both in her case were true.

"Cheryl, you need to slow your roll. We need to discuss this."

"Why? There is no discussion needed. I am not keeping this child, end of discussion." He grabbed her arm.

"Stop it," Cheryl screamed. "You lay up with some other bitch, fuck me occasionally and now that I'm pregnant, you act like a caring husband! Fuck you!" she kept flailing her arms until she broke free from his grip.

"Stop acting like a child! We had sex, you are pregnant

and now, without consulting me, or even telling me, you are deciding to get rid of our child without even a second thought."

"Did you consult me before you started fucking some other woman! Let's see, that would be no!"

"You are fucking unbelievable, you know that?"

"And so are you," she shouted back. She stormed upstairs and he went into his office. Suddenly he came upstairs, slammed the door open, startling her. He walked over to her and pulled her from the chair.

"You will not get rid of this child, do you understand me?"

"Or what? I'm not keeping this baby, end of story."

"No. Wrong answer. You won't speak to me any kind of way, do I make myself clear?" he said as he slammed her into the wall.

"If you get rid of my child, you will be sorry." He gave her enough of a shove that she fell backwards into the chair.

Two weeks after that doctor's appointment she awoke to the sun shining bright. She had not meant to sleep this long. She needed to be ready for her day. She went into the master bedroom and noticed that the bed was already made. It was past eleven so Kevin must already be gone to the office. She went downstairs and noticed there was no coffee, which could only mean one thing. He didn't stay there last night. Kevin loved his morning coffee. The fact that none was made meant that he was having coffee elsewhere that morning.

Chapter 35

She walked into the appointment by herself. She couldn't even bring herself to tell Dee about this mess. Just as she walked in, she walked out an hour later, by herself. She was there for blood work, which took much longer than it should have, but it gave her the opportunity to think things through. She thought about the ups and downs of having this child, she couldn't believe she was rethinking her decision. If nothing else, this child would know that it would be loved just like Donnell and Kayla.

She walked in and Kevin was waiting in the dining room.

"Where have you been?" She continued like she had not heard a word. She went upstairs.

"I said where in the hell have you been? Answer me!" He demanded. She continued walking.

"You better answer me!" he said from the bottom of the stairs.

"None of your business," she shouted back.

"Who in the hell do you think you are!"

"Whatever, Kevin."

She heard his heavy footsteps behind her but she kept walking.

"Who the fuck do you think you are?" he said while grabbing her arm.

"Get the hell off of me!" She shouted and walked into the bathroom and shut the door. The door came flying open.

"Who…!" He had slapped her twice before she could even register a thought.

"Get off of me!" she said while pushing back against him.

"I'm going to ask you again, where have you been?"

He had grabbed her hair and was yanking her backwards as she tried to cover her face.

"None of your fucking business."

"Really? Let me take a wild guess. Did you get rid of the baby?"

"What if I did?"

"Did you?" he shouted.

"Fuck you," she shouted back.

He hit her so hard that she flew backwards against the wall. She scrambled to steady herself.

"You better answer me, or so help me."

"If you really want to know, call a private investigator."

"I already did you bitch, and he followed your ass to the clinic. You got rid of my child even when I told you not to." He punched her in the face.

"What? You are crazy. Following me around?"

"Because your trifling ass can't be trusted!"

He punched her so hard that her head hit the wall and she saw stars. She slumped down to the floor. She woke up in the bathroom, not realizing where she was. She got up and looked into the mirror. She had a small cut on the side of her head and a small knot under her eye. She knew she was in trouble and nothing that she could do in this marriage would resolve the issue of Kevin being a man with a problem, namely her.

Chapter 36

"Hello?" her voice quivered.

"Hello my sweet."

"Do you know who this is?" she asked.

"Of course, I told you I would never forget you, Cheryl."

She started crying.

"Honey what's wrong?"

"He, I mean, we…he. I need to get out of here, can I come see you?"

"Sure but what's the matter. Do you need me to come and get you?"

"No, I'll come to you." She stopped crying long enough to get directions again. She got dressed and realized that she needed to cover up the marks as best she could. Makeup could only hide so much; hopefully glasses would hide the rest.

She walked into his office and waited while the pretty young receptionist checked in with him. She asked her to follow her into the back. "Shut the door please," Matthew said when she entered.

"Very cute young lady."

"Yes, but not gorgeous like the woman in front of me."

"You're much too kind." She said, while holding her head down.

"Take off your glasses, stay a while." She instantly

started to cry.

"What's wrong?" he asked as he came over to her, trying to lift her face with his hand.

"I'm pregnant." He gathered her in his arms. He pulled her glasses off and saw the bruise.

"How in the hell did that happen."

"He hit me. He thinks I had an abortion and he slapped me around a little bit."

"A little bit? That Motha…"

"Don't…he didn't mean to do it."

"Do not defend him to me."

"I'm not," she whimpered.

"Yes you are. He means it and you can't tell me he doesn't. Why else would you try and cover the bruises up?"

Her hand went to the place on her face and she tried to turn from him.

"It's okay, Cheryl. I'm here."

He took her into his arms and held her close.

"I'm sorry," she said, while pulling away from him.

"Nothing to be sorry about. What are you going to do about the baby?"

"I am going to have it. I couldn't go through with the abortion. No matter how I feel about him, I couldn't murder an innocent child. This child doesn't deserve to be put to death because it was conceived this way."

"What do you mean?"

"Nothing."

"No, not nothing. What do you mean?"

"I shouldn't have said anything," she said.

"But you did. Now tell me. Does he force you to have sex with him?"

She started bouncing her leg.

"Answer me."

"Kinda."

"The answer is either yes or no."

"Sometimes?"

"How often? Don't protect him," Matthew said.

"I'm not." After a short pause, she continued. "I don't know how many times."

"So if you don't sleep with him, he rapes you?"

"No."

"Yes Cheryl."

"I'm his wife for God sakes."

"When a woman says no, or indicates no, and a man does it anyway, it's called rape. So he rapes you."

She bolted from the chair. "Stop saying that. I'm his wife and I should be willing whenever he says. That is my responsibility as a wife."

"Bullshit!" he shouted.

"Let me explain, he does..."she spoke softly

"Stop it!"

"Stop what?"

"Protecting him. He doesn't deserve anything from you but a police report."

"I won't do that," she yelled back. Suddenly the door opened.

"Mr. Perry is everything ok?" the receptionist asked.

"I'm sorry Karen, yes, everything is fine." She closed the door again. Cheryl got up to leave and Matthew stepped in front of her.

"Look Cheryl. Sit down for a minute. I don't like seeing you like this. From the first night I saw you, and the way he was dogging you, I didn't like it. It took all I had not to run up on that nigga."

"Don't do this."

"Do what? Tell you how much I care for you. Tell you how I can't get you out of my mind. Tell you that I know you have feelings for me too. Tell you that ever since that kiss we shared, I have wanted you. I have wanted to make love to you, to hold you, to protect you."

"Stop it! Just stop it."

"Let me help you. Let me help you leave him. Come with me. You won't have to raise your children alone. I can help you."

He placed his hand on her stomach. She slapped it

175

away.

"You don't know a damn thing about me, let alone my children. You have no idea."

"Well tell me what I need to know."

She stood again to leave.

"I should not have come here. This was a mistake."

Matthew blocked her path.

"Please move."

"No, I can't'," Matthew said. She moved to his left and so did he.

"Why are you doing this?"

"Because I care about you."

"Whatever. How can you care for a person you don't even know. What is this really about? Sex? Do you want to have sex with me? Okay, come on? Let's do it."

She started unbuttoning her blouse.

He walked back behind his desk.

"Cheryl, stop it. If I had wanted sex, you wouldn't have left me that night when we kissed. Right now, I know you are going through some things, and I want to be your friend, nothing more, but in time, yes, I want to explore the possibilities. Look at me, I care for you and for right now, that will be enough to hold me. Whenever you need me, I will be there for you. Take this."

He reached in his desk and held out another business card. "Every number that I use is on this card. Use them whenever you need me."

She took the card and placed it in her pocket. He leaned forward, taking her hand in his.

"I mean it, just call me and I will be there, no questions asked." He touched her face and then drew his hand away quickly "Let's sit down and discuss how you could get this man out of your life."

"Do you know a hit man?" she said.

"I might," he said.

"Jeez, I'm only kidding," she said through a half smile.

Chapter 37

Kevin was home fuming. He knew she went to get an abortion, the P.I. told him that, and now she was nowhere to be found. It turned his stomach to know that Cheryl would bear his next child and not Rebecca. No matter, he would deal with that later.

Cheryl stopped by Dee's house and told her about her conversation with Matthew.

"You do know that Kevin will kill you if he finds out you are cheating on him."

"What? Who said anything about cheating? I haven't slept with the man."

"No, but he is not your husband and you are sharing things with him that you should be sharing with your husband. Mainly how you feel about this child. I'm your girl, if you need anyone to talk to, you talk to me."

"Dee, you just don't know."

"Then tell me."

"Kevin, well, he is becoming more violent. Anything sets him off. On a weekly basis, hell sometimes daily. It's getting worse. Look at my face, he did this today. He wants me to carry this child and he doesn't even know how to keep his hands to himself. He asks me for a divorce and now all of a sudden, he wants to be a father. Give me a break."

"So what are you going to do?"

"I am going to keep this child, but I will leave before it's born. I can't keep going through this. I just can't."

Both women started to cry and Dee tried to comfort her friend.

Still sitting in the living room floor with her friend, Cheryl wiped her eyes and stood and headed for the door.

Dee grabbed her friend and hugged her, "I'm here for you girl, no matter what. Just be careful when it comes to your friend."

Cheryl broke the embrace, "What do you mean by that?

"I mean, you know, your friend might want something other than friendship."

Cheryl backed away, "See where your mind automatically goes."

"No, I just mean, I know how men are." Dee said holding her hands up defensively.

"And how are they?" Cheryl said with her arms folded

"They will say what you want to hear, and then they want the panties."

"For your information, little miss know it all, he only wants to be my friend. I even offered myself to him and he was offended that I would even think he was like that. Do you have so little faith in me?" Cheryl said.

Dee blew out a breath before speaking "I didn't mean it like that."

"Yes you did. You think I am some helpless baby, who can't distinguish between good and evil. Well I will have you know that I can distinguish between my friends and someone who is jealous."

"Jealous? Jealous of who...you? Please. You think I want to be you? You, who has a husband that cheats on you, whose husband calls you names, whose husband beats her ass and comes and goes as he pleases? Yeah, no thanks." Dee said without taking a breath.

Let Me Just Say This

Cheryl opened the door and let it swing open.

Chapter 38

Cheryl walked in the house and walked by Kevin like she didn't see him. She did notice that his face was tight.

"Care to tell me where you have been?"

"Nope."

"Oh really. You're going to say that to me?" he said but she continued past him.

She went into the library and wanted to read. Something that always calmed her down and boy did she need something to settle the nerves. She was cried out, pissed off and tired.

"We need to talk about a few things." Kevin said as he walked into the library.

"We don't need to talk about anything."

"Yes we do. We need to discuss what you are going to do about being pregnant. I think…"

"Oh, you think. Isn't that rich? Well I will tell you what. No need for you to think about anything. Things are already taken care of."

"And what does that mean?"

"Just like it sounds." She stood to leave the library.

"Stop talking in riddles and tell me what the hell is going on."

"I don't need to tell you shit! You never tell me anything. Now you wanna be all up in my face, because you want to be a daddy. How about you be a daddy to the kids you already have! Screw you Kevin. You weren't acting like you wanted to be a daddy a month ago. You the one acting like you a single man. You barely even come home anymore. You could give a flying fuck about me, this baby or the kids.

Kevin's voice came out as a shriek.

"How dare you try and put the destruction of this marriage on me!"

"And why not?" she asked gasping, "You are out there with another woman. Not once have I ever thought about cheating on you. God knows I could have, so many times before, but did I, no, I stayed faithful. Why? Because I thought that if I did, you would see just how lucky your stupid ass was to have someone like me. Boy was I wrong. You only care about one thing, and that is you and that bitch you are screwing."

Kevin lunged at her, catching her off guard. They fell to the floor with him on top of her.

"Don't you ever call her that again? Do you hear me?"

"You're crazy," she screamed.

"I sure am," his hands tightened around her neck. She fought to keep him from tightening his grip. "You fucking bitch!" he shouted.

Suddenly his hands left her neck and he stood. She staggered to her feet, holding her neck and coughing.

"I won't let you do this again, I won't."

She ran for the phone on the desk.

"Who do you think you're calling?"

"Get away from me."

He pulled the jack from the wall, and grabbed her by the hair.

"Stop it!"

He slapped her hard across her face. She tried running from the room and shutting the door, but he was right there with her. By the time he had finished her eyes were swollen.

"I suggest you think the next time you get your ass on your shoulders," he said, breathing hard. "If you think I will stand around and let you come and go as you please, you are sadly mistaken; furthermore, if you even think about killing my child, I will do the same to you. Do you understand me? Do you?"

She lay there in a heap on the floor. She heard him throwing glasses and slamming things in the kitchen. She heard him enter the garage. She was hopeful he was leaving. She dragged herself onto the bed and closed her eyes.

Night had fallen and she finally woke up. Her head was killing her and the lights were not on in the house. She got up and felt around in the dark. She walked into the bathroom and turned on the lights. The lights illuminated all of the flowers in the room. This certainly was not going to stop her from calling the cops on his sorry ass. No matter what he did this time, she was not putting up with this anymore.

She heard a noise downstairs. "Sweetheart, are you awake?" he called.

She went back and climbed into bed.

"You need to eat," he said as he walked in with a tray of food.

"I'm not hungry."

"The baby might be," he said. "So eat."

He sat the tray down when he heard the doorbell ring.

"Just eat, I'll get it."

She stared at the tray of food as long as she could then pushed it to the floor.

Kevin came running up the stairs.

"Are you alright?" he asked, unaware that Dee was behind him.

"What the fuck happened? What did he do to you?"

Dee wrapped her arms around her. Cheryl looked at Kevin then turned her head.

"Nothing. I fell downstairs. You know with the pregnancy and all, I got dizzy."

Dee looked at her and leaned in for a hug. She whispered, "Why are you protecting him?" she looked away.

Dee got up and ran up on Kevin, "You piece of shit. You did this didn't you? I'm calling the cops."

"Sweetie, you will be so embarrassed when Cheryl tells them what really happened."

"Just look at her," she screamed and came back to Cheryl, "she looks like she went three rounds with you."

"Dee, I'm fine. I'm a little tired. I'll call you tomorrow," she said, while trying to convince her friend, that she had it all under control. Kevin came and grabbed her by the arm.

"You need to leave," he said sweetly. "The doctor said she needs to rest."

As he led her downstairs, she could hear Dee, "I know you did this, and she is too scared to say anything. How could you hit her, knowing she's pregnant?"

"I don't know what you are talking about. I will tell Cheryl that you will call her later, ok? Bye." He pushed her in the back and slammed the door.

Chapter 39

Dee couldn't leave things with Cheryl like that. After an hour, she calmed down enough to drive to Cheryl's house and what she found broke her heart into even smaller pieces. She got home and as she walked into the door, she saw a card lying on the floor. "This must have fallen out of her pocket." She said as she leaned to pick it up.

She knew she shouldn't but she didn't know what else to do. She called Matthew and after introducing herself. She told him what she saw when she got to Cheryl's house.

"Look, I don't know if I should be telling you this, but if Cheryl trusts you I guess I can too. He beat her up so bad this time, she was in bed and her face was almost unrecognizable. She was in bed and he didn't want me to see her. You say you are her friend, right? So how can we get her away from him? He is going to end up killing her." She listened intently as Matthew hatched a plan to get her away from Kevin. She knew that the only way to do it was to force her hand. She let Matthew finish telling her the plan and then she made that call to Cheryl. Cheryl told her that Kevin was asleep and she didn't want to wake him but Dee convinced her to listen. When she was confident enough that Cheryl would follow the plan she hung up and went into her guest room to get it ready for her new roommate.

Cheryl hung up and immediately called her parents to ask if the kids could stay with them for a while. They agreed so she got up and packed a bag so she could leave first thing in the morning. She couldn't let him see her with the bag so she hurried downstairs and threw it in the truck. Coming back into the house, she was confronted by Kevin but she told him she just needed some fresh air.

The next morning, she got up, showered and left the house while Kevin was still asleep. As her truck pulled from the garage, Kevin stood at the living room window.

It was nice just to sit and talk to Dee and Matthew. Of course, they wanted her to call the police, but she wasn't going to do that. She had agreed to leave, so that is all that mattered. Matthew made some arrangements for her to stay at a hotel and Dee agreed to pick up the kids and bring them to her. Matthew then arranged for one of his cars to take her, since he didn't want her driving the truck she had.

"Too easy to trace," he said. "Look, I won't let anything hurt you, do you understand?" She raised her face to his and he kissed her gently.

She drove home and slept for the rest of the day. She was so tired, even after getting out of the shower she decided to lay back down.

Chapter 40

Kevin came up the stairs in a rage. She looked at him and tried to diffuse the situation.

"I'm leaving in two days. You can have the house and the cars. I only want the kids and my things. I just can't take this anymore."

Her heart was pounding so hard, she knew he should be able to hear it. Suddenly she wasn't feeling good about the situation and got up from the bed. She started down the stairs only to have him hot on her heels.

"Wait one damn minute. You sleep all day, and suddenly you wake up, tell me that you are leaving and that's it. What has gotten into you?"

"Have you not noticed my eyes?" she said as she reached the bottom of the stairs.

"Who have you been talking to? Who's been filling your head with this nonsense? Dee?"

"You have, remember. You wanted a divorce, you asked me so I am giving it to you."

"Yes, but that was before I knew about the baby. We need to be together until this child is born."

Things were not going as she had planned. She thought he would be happy to hear that she wouldn't block the divorce. She was supposed to tell him that as long as he let her leave, she would share joint custody.

"Look, stop for a minute and let's just talk."

She opened the closet door, got the luggage and started back for the stairs.

"Stop and listen to me" he said, grabbing her arm.

"Don't you fucking put your hands on me again, or I swear I will call the police."

"Where were you today? I tried calling you a hundred damn times, you didn't answer."

"I turned it off."

"So, where were you?"

"Out."

"With who?"

"With people who care about me."

"Then tell me this, why do you smell like a man's cologne?

"I don't smell anything, and neither do you."

"Oh, is that what Matthew wears."

"What…what are you talking about?" she stuttered. "You must be losing your mind, I don't smell anything."

"Oh, am I crazy to know that Dee called you with someone named Matthew on the other line and you met with him today. Yep, I heard you make your little plans yesterday, you dumb trick. You play miss innocent, but really you been out here the whole time, fucking around with some other man behind my back."

"You are something else Kevin. I haven't been the one cheating, you have. The only person I've been fucking is your trifling ass."

He grabbed her and shoved her into the wall.

"I believe I told you what would happen if I thought you were screwing around on me. Didn't I?"

She pushed against him and slapped him hard.

"I've done nothing with no one but you. Only you. You are the one cheating. Leaving me here with the kids all the time. I have put up with this shit for over three years, coming home with her nasty ass perfume lingering on you like a cheap suit. No more. I'm leaving. You can have her. I hate you! I hate you! How long did you think I would put up with this crap? You coming and going as you please and hitting me. I hope she is worth it, because you are about to lose everything you love."

"What is that supposed to mean?"

"It means, you lose, Kevin, your wife, your kids and this baby."

"Oh, you think you are taking my kids away from me?"

"You don't think I'm leaving them here do you?"

Kevin screamed, "You think I'm going to let you take my kids, you are totally crazy."

"Oh, I am not only taking them, but since you can't keep your hands to yourself, I am going for full custody."

He grabbed her before she had a chance to move.

"What! You think I am going to let you take my kids, you been out there all day, fucking some man, waltz up in here and say you are leaving and taking my kids."

"I want them around a man who knows how to treat women, because you obviously don't."

"You aren't taking them anywhere, you slut. Did your new little boyfriend put you up to this? What, you have to suck his little dick? What the fuck did I tell you I would do to you? Huh? You fucking hypocrite." He shoved her hard and she fell to the floor. "You probably been fucking him every chance you got."

"Get off of me!"

"When I am good and damn ready I will get off of your whoring ass. Is that who you were with today?"

He slapped her on the side of her head.

"Answer me, were you?"

He got up and dragged her along with him to the window.

"Is he outside somewhere waiting for you? Huh? That nigga ain't nothing but a punk."

"What…like you." She shouted, while pulling away from him.

"Get out of my house."

"Gladly." She didn't bother to pick up the luggage; she grabbed her purse and headed for the door.

"Don't you ever come back here!" He yelled from the den.

"You think I would dare step back into hell! You can go there your damn self." She shouted.

"I'll meet you there," he shouted back. She stopped in the foyer.

"You know what?" She said while walking back towards him, "You hit me, degrade me, call me every name but my God given one and I have never done anything to you. I am the mother of your children and this child I'm carrying."

The tears started to fall." You never loved me, only yourself. You loved the idea of having someone you could control. But no more. I won't be here to push around anymore. You can have that trick you been seeing, just tell her she better have a good lawyer on retainer, cause you are going to need one."

She turned to leave, not realizing how close he was to her. As she opened the front door, he slammed it and shoved her into it. He slapped her so hard in the back of the head that her head hit the door then grabbed her by the hair. She flailed her arms wildly, trying to grab his hands then bolted for the office.

"You fucking bitch. I will kill you."

She reached the office but couldn't find the phone. He came in after her, closing the door behind him.

"You bitch. Do you think..." he took deliberate steps toward her. "That anyone..." inching closer, "Will put up with this shit!"

He grabbed her by the hair and pulled her towards him.

"Get off of me!"

"When I'm ready." He back-handed her across the face. "Let's just see if he will want you after I am finished with you."

After what seemed like hours, Kevin rolled off of her. He had done every unimaginable thing to her. She had long given up the fight. The more she fought the more pain he inflicted on her. She couldn't see from one eye and her body was tender.

After Kevin finished with her he said, "let's see if he wants your ass now."

He stood and looked down at her.

"Get out of my fucking sight," he sneered.

She stood and steadied herself against his mahogany desk. She put her hand to her mouth, hoping that it would stop the liquid that threatened to spill from it. It hadn't worked. She started to vomit. She felt something running down her leg and looked; realizing it was her own blood. Her back was sore; her head felt like a rock had been thrown at it. Her hands were scratched, and her breasts were sore and tender. She could barely lift her arms. Her neck felt as if he had chewed it raw. Her clothes lay in tatters all over his office floor. She tried walking to the door but it hurt so much that she fell to her knees. He sucked his teeth and stepped over her body; leaving her there, like a wounded deer struck down by a speeding car. She vomited again and again. Her stomach started to cramp, and she fell to her knees, crying for the pain to go away. She pulled herself up and made it upstairs. He was snoring so loudly she knew he wouldn't wake up anytime soon. She moved as quickly as she could, covering herself with a lounging dress she found in the closet. The fabric made her body hurt more. She made her way back downstairs and found her purse along with her cell phone. She took his keys from the hook in the foyer and hurried to the garage. She climbed into his car, a feat in itself. Once she was clear of the driveway, she pulled the cell from her pocket and called Matthew, he would meet her at the mall parking lot. Luckily it was Sunday so it would be empty by now.

Matthew arrived first and noticed a car pulling up. Immediately he recognized Cheryl. She opened the door and he noticed that she was struggling to get out. He raced over to her door, and looked at her.

"Please, don't ask any questions right now. I just need you to take me home."

He walked beside her and put her inside his truck. He drove to his house and helped her inside and up the stairs. He called for his housekeeper, and asked her to find a robe and bring some water and find the aspirin. He tried getting her to call the police, but she flatly refused. He walked her into the bathroom and he turned the shower on, as she requested. She climbed in and let the water slide down her sore body, as well as the tears.

She heard Matthew going through her purse and heard him on the phone with someone.

"Cheryl, are you alright in there? Cheryl?"

There was no answer so he opened the door and Cheryl was standing in the shower. The bathroom was fogged up; he walked toward the open shower. She looked up at him and he climbed in with her. She began to sob uncontrollably. He took her in his arms.

"Your clothes," she said.

"They are only clothes. I'm here honey. I'm here with you."

She wrapped her arms around him and continued to cry. They stood like that for a while. He pulled her up into his arms and carried her into his bedroom. He laid her down and covered her. He stripped his clothes off and climbed in beside her and gathered her up into his arms. She continued to cry until she fell asleep.

The police banged on the door until Kevin came downstairs. He opened it, only for the white policeman to announce that he was under arrest. Maybe he shouldn't have drunk the last of the scotch, because he felt as though he was sucking on a cotton ball. He was stunned. He was led out of his house in handcuffs. The neighbors were truly getting a show; with all of the cop cars out there you would have thought the sniper was on the loose again. He started calling for Cheryl, but she never came from wherever she was.

Kevin called the house once he got to the police station, but no one answered. He called his boy, but of course he wouldn't be home. He finally called Rebecca and explained that he needed a lawyer because they were accusing him of assaulting Cheryl.

Cheryl was nowhere to be found, so he knew the charge couldn't be right. If only she would answer the phone and straighten this shit out. Rebecca was there with the lawyer in no time. The police explained that Cheryl had called in a report, however since they could not reach her to come into the station, they would release him until she was located. He and Rebecca went to his house and he was horrified at the site. The den was a mess. The liquor cabinet was open and two bottles of scotch were drained. He went into the office and the foul smell filled his lungs when he walked in. Torn clothes lay everywhere, the door was broken from the hinges and his chair was pushed over and there was blood on the wall and carpet. There was broken glass everywhere.

Someone must have broken into the house, was the first thought that came to Kevin's mind. He called the police and told them his house had been broken into and to report that his car had been stolen. They came over and took a report and in less than two hours, they called him to tell him that his Lo Jack system had tracked down his missing car. When he arrived at the mall parking lot, the policeman told him that it didn't appear to be stolen. He wondered who his wife might have met because the doors were locked. The cops said he could take his car so he told Rebecca she could go and he would meet her back at his house. Then he noticed it, her wedding ring.

Oh, out here hoeing around, are we, you will be dealt with whenever you get home.

Cheryl began to stir beside Matthew, who was snoring

lightly. As she began opening her eyes, a terrible pain shot through her, like a bolt of lightning.

"Cheryl, are you alright?" she heard him ask.

She couldn't speak because the pain was getting worse. She began to curl herself into a ball, hoping that it would ease the pain. She reached out and grabbed his arm.

"Cheryl!" he said a little louder.

"Oh God!" She screamed out. This pain was nothing like child birth. Matthew bolted up.

"Cheryl, talk to me. What's wrong?"

"It hurts! It hurts!" is all she could mutter.

"What? What hurts? Baby you have to tell me."

"Matthew please, please make it stop!" She grasped his arm and held her stomach. She knew exactly what was happening.

"What? What? Honey please, you have to tell me."

"Matthew," she gasped, "I think I'm losing the baby!"

Kevin arrived back at his house and saw Rebecca's car parked in the driveway. "What?" he asked her, when she gave him a disapproving look.

"You did this Kevin?"

"What are you talking about?" he said as he found some vodka and poured himself a drink.

"Do you really think you need to be drinking? These are her clothes and they smell like the cologne you were...I have seen her wear this before." Rebecca began to pace. "Did you and her have an argument?"

"Look, as far as I know, Cheryl has not been here yet. So I have no clue as to what you are talking about."

Kevin's phone rang and he was more agitated when he hung up. He took another swallow from his glass, drained and refilled it.

Rebecca asked if anything was wrong and who was on the phone, but he declined telling her. He instead told her that he needed to go out for a few minutes. He typed the directions into his GPS system and headed in that direction. Kevin pulled up in front of the office complex. There were no other cars around except for a couple of delivery vans. He had to make sure not to walk close to either one of them; someone could be lurking inside. He approached the building; having the uneasy feeling that someone was watching. He rode the elevator to the third floor like he had been instructed. When he stepped off, he noticed lights at the far end of the hall. He wasn't going to be a punk about this.

Kevin stepped from the elevator and called out. When no answer came he continued to the end of the hallway.

"Let's skip the hellos and get to it. What the fuck do you want?" Kevin asked as he found the office where the light came from and saw him sitting behind his desk.

"Don't you want to at least know who I am?" Matthew asked.

"I already know. I thought I recognized your voice. You called my house a while back, right? When all along you have been fucking my wife. She is probably with you right now, isn't she? She thinks I don't know about you and her. I heard your little plan the other day. Her making plans to come and see you. Is this where she comes? What, you can't spring for a cheap hotel room?"

"Partna, you got it all wrong. I am not sleeping with your wife, I'm only her friend. She needed someone to listen to her. Someone who wouldn't put his hands around her throat or hit her whenever she had something to say."

"My marriage is none of your business. I don't know what she has been filling your head with, but what goes on in my marriage, is my business". Matthew stood from behind the desk and moved around to where Kevin was standing.

"Does that include raping her?"

"You better watch yourself. You don't know who you are fucking with." Kevin said.

Matthew inched closer to Kevin.

"Oh, but I do. You like to hit women, and then degrade them, and then you take what isn't yours to take."

Matthew and Kevin stood face to face.

"You might want to back up partna." Kevin said.

"Naw, I think I'm right where I need to be," Matthew said. "Cheryl is my friend and I don't like my friends being treated like this. She came to me earlier and could barely move."

"Why are you telling me this?"

"You need to know what you did, didn't go unnoticed."

"I've already told you, that what goes on in my marriage is none of your concern."

"Oh, but you see, it is. When I looked at her, with her eyes swollen, and bruises everywhere, it became my business." Matthew bumped past Kevin.

"Oh, are you trying to scare me?"

"No nigga, I'm not trying to scare you. Right now I am just trying to get you to feel what she must feel like, right before you hit her."

Matthew raised his arm, causing Kevin to step back.

"Why don't you just let Cheryl go and let her find someone who will treat her like she ought to be treated?"

"Oh, is that someone you? Did she tell you that I asked her for a divorce and she begged me not to leave her? Yep, cried like a baby. Then she fucked me real good, that's probably when she got pregnant. She is nothing but a conniving bitch, which will stop at nothing to get some weak ass brotha, like you, to believe she is so innocent. Did she tell you that she fucked me so good last night, that she had me hollering? I guess she didn't," he said with a laugh, "That bitch sucked my dick like a newborn on the tittie."

Matthew grabbed Kevin and had a handful of his shirt.

"Nigga, I suggest you let me go. Someone knows I came here and now that I have your name, it wouldn't be hard to report you." Matthew gave him enough of a shove to send Kevin backwards.

"Get the fuck out of here!" Matthew shouted. "Oh, but one more thing, give her the divorce and anything she wants. But this, between me and you, this isn't over partna, count on it."

Kevin was shaken. Who in the hell does he think he is? He is only the man fucking her, I'm her damn husband. I will gladly give her ass a divorce. I have been trying to do this shit for weeks, and here she got this dude thinking I'm the one who doesn't want it. God only knows what she has been telling this fool and this nigga got the nerve to be threatening me. Oh Cheryl, you will be dealt with.

Chapter 41

Kevin walked in the house and Rebecca was putting the finishing touches on cleaning up his mess.

"What happened? Where did you go?" She asked.

"Just stay out of it!" he snapped and walked into the kitchen to get a glass of water. She came behind him, grabbed him and spun him around.

"Don't you ever, as long as you are black, tell me to stay out of something! If I ask you a damn question, I expect an answer! I expect the same courtesy I give you. Do you understand me? You leave me here, cleaning up your raggedy shit, I'm worried half to death that you could be sitting in jail and you have the fucking nerve to tell me to stay out of it! I don't fucking think so!"

"I am sorry. I know you care. I'm under a lot of pressure, with being arrested and not knowing where in the hell Cheryl is. I didn't mean to yell at you."

Matthew got lost in the words that Kevin said, "she cried like a baby, begged me not to leave her." His cell phone brought him out of the trance. He had called Dee to tell her what happened and she was calling him back. Of course she was on her way to the hospital. He got back to the hospital to see Dee, who was sitting with an older couple. Dee introduced them as Cheryl's parents. The father rose and shook his hand, the mother; she gave a disapproving look and turned her head.

Kevin walked into the emergency room and greeted Cheryl's parents. He glanced to his right and saw Matthew sitting there. Matthew saw him and it was more than he could bear. He ran up on him and starting swinging. Matthew caught Kevin with a blow to the side of his head. Kevin managed to get to his feet and you would have thought the twelfth round of a championship bout had just started. Security had to be called and the two men were separated.

"Officer, this man came at me for no reason." Kevin said. "I came here to be with my wife."

"Bullshit! How are you coming to visit your wife and you have her with you?" Matthew said, pointing in the direction of Rebecca. "Your wife is in the back, beaten black and blue and just had a miscarriage because of you."

"Look, I have no idea what he is talking about. I want this man arrested."

"You might want to rethink that buddy. You might end up in the same cell."

After walking Kevin down the hall, the other officer addressed Matthew.

"Is what he said true? Did you attack that man?"

"Look, I know I was wrong. But you should see what he did to her. She lost a baby because of him. She doesn't deserve this shit. I care for that woman, as a friend, and if he thinks that is going to change, he is sadly mistaken."

Kevin was close enough to hear the last statement.

"Dude, she is still married to me. Don't get it twisted. She is my wife, not yours. Keep your comments to yourself."

"Or what?" Matthew said, side-stepping the officer.

"Don't think this shit will happen again," Kevin said while straightening his shirt

Matthew started towards Kevin.

"Or what nigga? I'm not Cheryl, you punk ass mothafucka. Try that shit with me and you won't be able to lift your hands to hold your dick while you pee, let alone hit someone."

Kevin tried going around the security guard.

"That's enough you two," The officer said.

"I'm straight," Matthew said to the officer.

Kevin walked back towards the nurse's station.

"I'm here to see my wife."

The officer pulled Matthew to the side.

"Is what you said true? Did he assault her?"

"All I know is, when I saw her yesterday she wasn't bruised and shit like she is today."

The officer raised his eyebrows.

"Look, don't get it twisted, like I said, I'm only her friend. Nothing more."

"Well, if that is true, you need to talk her into pressing charges." Matthew walked away and sat down. A nurse called to him. He went to her and she informed him that Cheryl wanted to see him.

Matthew pulled the chair closer to the bed.

"Feeling better?"

"Much" she said sleepily. "I'm sorry."

"Don't be. If it was meant to be…"

The nurse walked back in and told her that her husband was here. Immediately her heart began to race. Matthew noticed her hands become sweaty.

"I'll be outside," Matthew said and gave her hand a squeeze.

Kevin walked past Matthew and brushed up against him. He looked at her and she could tell by the twitch in his jaw that he was fuming.

"I lost the baby because of you." She blurted out.

"I have no idea what you are talking about." Before she could say anything else, the nurse said the doctor would be in shortly. Kevin leaned down over her and her breathing quickened.

"Care to know that your little boyfriend will be arrested by the end of the day."

"He is not my boyfriend." she said.

"Oh, that's what you say. Anyway, he attacked me, right here in the lobby, everyone saw it, and I am pressing charges."

"Attacked you for what? What did you do to him?"

"Isn't that sweet? You are sticking by your man, more than you ever did for me. I guess since you have been fucking him behind my back, you got your priorities twisted."

"That is not true. I haven't slept with him. I am not like you."

"No matter. No man attacks another man over some chic he hasn't screwed. He will be sorry though."

"Are you blind, or just stupid? Can't you see that my eye is swollen and these cuts didn't get there all by themselves? Maybe you are the one that I should be sending to jail." she said.

"Why you little..."

"Mr. and Mrs. Goldman, I'm Dr. Thornton. First my apology on your loss."

Kevin spoke up. "Thank you, sometimes things happen beyond our control." She sucked her teeth.

Yes, well don't let that deter you from trying again," he said. She spoke up quickly, "Oh, we won't be trying again, it was for the best."

The doctor continued. "Now, I need to discuss some things with the both of you." She interrupted him again.

"Can he leave please?"

"Uh, sure. If that is what you want." Kevin tried to protest but the doctor was already escorting him out of the room. As the doctor walked in, she could see the expression written all over his face.

"Doctor, first let me say. No matter what you think, I am not pressing charges, nor do I need to go into a shelter. They have already talked to me and I told them my answer then."

"Oh, so you have heard it before, so when will you listen, when you have a broken arm, or when he puts your eye out. Maybe it's when he puts a bullet in you. There is no reason you should have had a miscarriage because you have had two other pregnancies that went to term. Your baby didn't have to die." Why was he being so harsh to her? "I have seen women in your predicament before and the outcome is always the same, they are either seriously injured or end up as the lead story on the local news."

"Stop it; I don't want to hear anymore."

"You need to hear this. Do you realize you could have bled to death? Your uterus was torn, that doesn't just happen. Did you also know that you have twenty three stitches in your perianal area? That doesn't just happen either, that is from brutal force, from being raped."

"No, I was in an accident a little while ago, and my stomach had been bothering me ever since, and my husband likes it a little rough, that's all."

"Oh, is that what you normally tell people. That the bruises are from rough sex? What about the bruises we found on your back, what is that from? Please let someone help you."

"I would like to get some rest now," she said as she turned over.

Matthew left her room and noticed that this woman was hovering over Kevin like a moth to a flame. Kevin seemed to know this woman intimately, and was not trying to hide the fact.

Matthew spoke with Lynette before leaving the hospital.

Kayla came into the hospital with Donnell on her heels. Donnell went to speak with his grandparents. Kayla walked up to her dad.

"How could you? You did it again? Didn't you? I knew you would end up hurting her! She tried killing herself because of you, and here you are with this woman all over you. Are you happy? You took my dad from my mom?"

"Kayla that is enough!" Kevin screamed, causing

201

everyone to look in their direction.

"No, you hit her all the time. You think we don't hear you? We do!"

"That's enough young lady," Kevin said while grabbing her arm.

"What are you going to do, hit me too? Go ahead, but I will call the cops on your sorry ass!"

Kevin was nearing the end of his rope with her. Rebecca tried coaxing him away, but he pulled away from her.

"She's angry, let her be," Rebecca said.

"Better listen to your little girlfriend. Before she has to bail you out of jail."

"Stop acting like a spoiled little brat!"

"I will, as soon as you stop being a wife beater."

Before she could say another word, Kevin had slapped her. Donnell came running up to his father and slammed him against the hospital wall.

"Don't you ever touch her!" Donnell screamed.

"Well lookahere. If it isn't my punk ass son, trying to stick up for his little sister. I thought it would be the other way around, being that you're such a pussy," Kevin sneered.

Donnell started swinging and Kevin sidestepped him.

"Don't get your bitch ass hurt up in here," Kevin said.

Donnell connected with a punch to his face and blood poured from Kevin's nose. "You little..."

Lynette rounded the corner just as Rebecca was struggling to pull them apart. Donnell's shirt was torn and he had a busted lip. Kevin was holding his shirt to his bleeding nose.

"Don't you ever put your fucking hands on my sister again!"

"I'm your father nigga..."

"Oh, I wish you weren't. I also wish my father didn't beat my mom, but that isn't true either, is it? Put your hands on my sister or my mom again, and I will put a bullet in you."

Donnell said and stormed away. Lynette walked over and comforted Kayla.

"You should be ashamed of yourself," She said to Kevin.

"Who the fuck are you lady? You need to mind your own damn business," Kevin said.

"C'mon sweetie. Let's go see your mom," she said, leading Kayla down the hall.

When they arrived in Cheryl's room, Kayla ran to her bed and started crying. "I hate him! I hate him!" It truly broke Cheryl's heart. Lynette sat down and pulled Kayla down in the chair.

Matthew stood and said he needed to leave and get some fresh air. "I will be back later," he said and kissed Cheryl on the forehead. He walked to the elevators, got in and his anger overtook him. He punched the wall. When the doors opened, he saw Kevin standing there. Matthew exited and brushed past Kevin.

"Punk ass..." Before Kevin finished, Matthew had him pinned against the wall. "Partna, don't fucking press your luck. Don't take me for being overly generous. I will get rid of your punk ass and think nothing of it."

Matthew walked off before Kevin could respond.

Chapter 42

The cold air shocked Matthew. Had it been this cold earlier? He hopped into his car and headed towards the gym. He needed to work off some of this anger.

Kevin walked back into Cheryl's room to see Kayla talking with her mother. Kevin figured she must be telling Cheryl her version of what had just happened.

"Mom, why don't you just leave? You can't love him. You never smile, you never laugh like you used to. You are always sitting in your room and crying. Then you let him hit you all the time. You don't ever call the police, nothing. You tell me and Donnell not to let people hurt us, but you let dad do it every day. Why don't you take your own advice?"

Cheryl was surprised at what Kayla was saying, "Kayla, your dad is not a bad man. He has a temper and sometimes I push him too far, that's all. You should not have talked to him that way, it wasn't right. You need to apologize to him. Donnell also needs to apologize, that was very disrespectful."

"What about him. He disrespects you by beating you."

"Sweetie, don't get upset with our problems. You are only a teenager and one day you will understand the choices that grownups make when they think they are doing something right but it turns out all wrong."

"No I won't. I will never understand why you let him beat you up." Kayla got up and stormed from the room.

Kevin stood in the doorway, not believing what he had

just heard. She could have told Kayla a million different things, instead she had defended him. Why did she make him so angry? Cheryl could have been his soul mate, but she had become so needy. Was he actually like his father? Why was Cheryl able to push his buttons? Kevin walked in cautiously.

"I'm not here to argue. I just want you to grant me the divorce and I will be on my way. I have called the lawyer and have taken care of everything. Donnell and I just had it out, but he is still my child and I will take care of him, no matter what. I will pay for their school a year in advance, so you won't have to worry about that. If you want the truck, you can have it. I'm tired of the fighting."

"Are you saying all of this because you think I am going to have you thrown in jail?"

"Look, I'm doing this because I want to be happy. Ain't shit got to do with you making any threat."

"I'm not pressing charges. I just want you to get some help."

"I don't need anything but my divorce," Kevin said angrily.

"You are pathetic," she mumbled.

"Look, I didn't come in here for a fucking argument. See that is why you always got your ass beat. You don't know when to keep your fucking mouth shut."

"All I said…"

"Shut up!" he yelled a little too loud, causing the nurse to come running.

"I'm ok," Cheryl assured her.

Kevin continued, "Just do what I ask you to do. Just grant the divorce and you and your little boyfriend can ride off in the sunset."

"Like I said before, Matthew is just my friend. No matter what you think. You are the only one who brought someone else in this marriage. Whoever she is, I hope she doesn't make you mad like I always seemed to do. You just might end up in jail."

Kevin stormed out of the room.

Cheryl's head was spinning. What in the hell just happened? She was finally going to be free of him, free from the hell, and free to live her life as she pleased. What could she do? All she knew was being Mrs. Goldman, a wife and mother. How was she going to manage?

Chapter 43

Matthew worked out for almost two hours. Sparring was such a great release for him. Every blow was for her. Every punch was meant to take the pain away.

"Damn, what has got you so worked up?" his sparring partner asked.

"Nothing, just stressed."

"Over some chic?"

Matthew stopped long enough to give him a long hard stare. "No." He stopped sparring again and after a long pause said, "Ever been in a situation where you know what you need to do, but you don't know how to do it?"

"Yep, plenty of times."

"And?"

"And, your gut tells you what to do. The answer will become clear."

"Thanks."

"For?"

"For listening and taking a beating," Matthew said, giving his partner a quick shot to the gut. "I owe you lunch."

"Naw nigga, you owe me breakfast, dinner and a couple of snacks."

Matthew headed towards the sauna. The heat and the steam would relax the rest of his tension away. He walked in and let the steam take over. Before long he was thinking of Cheryl.

She sat next to him. Her smooth dark skin glistened

with beads of perspiration.

She rested her head back on the wall. His fingers gliding over her skin. His touch made her skin tingle. She was the most beautiful creature he knew. He stood before her, letting his towel drop from his waist. He knelt, wanting to taste her essence. His tongue licked her ankles slowly inching up behind her knee.

She loved this, and she moaned her pleasure. He kissed and licked the inside of her thighs, blowing small puffs where his tongue once was. He continued his journey to her secret garden. He tasted her sweetness and was turned on even more. He licked her, sucked her and caressed her. His tongue dove deep into her juicy abyss. His fingers played her button like a violin.

She came once, and then she came again. The more he tasted, the more he wanted. She moved away from his mouth but he wrapped his muscular arms around her thighs and pulled her back. He dove inside her again. Her moans filled the sauna. His manhood was solid. God he couldn't get enough of her. He needed to fill her.

He came up to her and kissed her hungrily. He kissed her ears, her neck, her shoulders, her breasts. He wanted her so badly. Let me in, baby, he whispered in her ear, "Let me in."

The knocking jolted him back into reality. Shit. It was only a dream. Hell, don't tell his penis that. He was willing, ready and able. Matthew walked slowly and opened the door. Two older women were waiting. They must have taken notice of the bulge under his towel.

"Oh, you can stay," one of them said with a wink. "We won't hurt you."

The other chimed in, "Unless you want us to." They shared a laugh.

"This is for one person and one person only," he said with a wink and smile.

"Lucky girl.'

"No, lucky me," He said and headed toward the shower.

He needed one badly, a nice cold one.

Cheryl woke in a panic.

"Someone really loves you," a voice said. "There were at least four dozen delivered."

She felt panicked and tried climbing out of bed.

"Whoa and where do you think you are going?"

"I have to get out of here."

"Sweetie, you need to rest."

"I can't. I need to get out of here." The nurse called for assistance.

"Please Mrs. Goldman, you need to calm down."

Cheryl was like a wild animal. The nurses were still struggling with her when Matthew arrived.

"What's wrong with her?" he asked coming to her bedside.

"Sir, we are not sure. She woke up like this." Cheryl looked at him pleadingly.

"They won't let me go. I can't stay here."

"It's only for one night. Then in the morning, I will come and get you and take you home."

"No, I won't stay here!" she was becoming hysterical. Dr. Thornton arrived.

"Don't you like Conchita? The food and the service can't be that bad, or is it her breath; you know she eats tons of garlic," he said jokingly.

"Can I just go home?"

"Tomorrow morning."

"No, now," she demanded.

"First thing in the morning you can be the first one out the doors. But for now, we just need to keep you for observation. Now, just lay back, take a deep breath and let Conchita keep you company. Her breath isn't that bad is it?"

Cheryl laid back and looked at the ceiling. She heard him ask to speak with Matthew.

"She will be fine. She just had a panic attack, which is

209

not uncommon given what she has been through. She could start having nightmares as well. I don't think she should have any more visitors."

"Was her husband here?"

"I can't tell you that, but as her friend, ask her to calm down, and rest. And that I will let her leave in the morning."

Matthew walked in and she tried to stop crying.

"It's ok. Go on and cry. I am here for you. Always remember that."

"No, you aren't," she whined.

"What do mean?"

"You said you would always be there for me. You weren't. You weren't there, when he dragged me to the window and.....he raped me. Oh Matthew, he raped me."

Matthew was cemented to the floor.

"I'm sorry," is all he could mutter. He climbed on the bed with her and gathered her in his arms. He spoke in a whisper, "I can't lose you. My mother fell in love with the wrong man and paid the price for it. I will not let you do the same. I will protect you with everything that I have. You are safe, safe in my arms and I will wrap my love and protection around you." He said as he smoothed down her hair and waited for her to fall asleep.

Chapter 44

Two years later the divorce was final. Thanks to Matthew, Cheryl learned that she is an important person. Matthew began teaching her how to box. The kids are in an adjustment period. Kayla stopped speaking to her father shortly after the miscarriage but now she is not talking to Cheryl either. Donnell moved in with his friends until he graduated and went off to college. Cheryl learned that Rebecca Hardy was the other woman after all the years of wondering. She was right under her nose the entire time.

She stopped by his office late one night to drop off some the folders with the contract that she found in her box with her important papers. She started to leave them on the desk out front, but heard voices, so decided to walk towards the back. There they were, him with his ass all up in the air and her legs wrapped around him like the snake that she was. Cheryl couldn't move. She had become a mute at that very moment.

"Whose is it Rebecca?" he asked as Cheryl looked on.

"Umm, didn't mean to interrupt you. Good Lord, I guess he didn't want to waste the money on a hotel, huh?" Cheryl said, "here are the papers I told you I would drop off."

"Now that you did, you can leave." He said as he yanked up his pants and tried to push his hard penis into his pants.

Cheryl looked past him and to the woman rising from

the desk. "You should be ashamed of yourself. Business manager and home wrecker. You are very talented."

"You can leave now," he said.

Cheryl continued talking to Rebecca, "Was there ever a time that you thought, umm, this is wrong. He is a married man, or are you just a tramp who couldn't find her own man?"

Rebecca was dressed and putting on her shoes.

"How dare you," she said while she was fixing her clothes.

"How dare me, you are the one with her legs stuck up in the air and wrapped around another woman's husband, who is also her boss."

Rebecca spoke fast, "You have a nerve, what the two of us do is none of your business."

"Well, we weren't even separated when he started this little affair, now were we honey? No wonder you didn't want to tell me who it was. Did you know that after being with you, he would come home and have sex with me too? Of course you didn't. You must think I am totally stupid. All the nights, you needed me. That nasty ass perfume lingered on you like a cheap suit. It was the first thing I smelled when you walked into the house. Oh, how about when he traveled, he always brought along a box of condoms. Oh, didn't think I knew that either. We didn't use them, so let me guess who they were for. Then one day I called you a bitch. My God, he flipped. Did you know he raped me and caused me to have a miscarriage? You got what you wanted, my husband. But don't get too secure, you're replaceable, isn't that right honey?"

"Get the hell out of here!" he growled at her.

"Gladly. You two deserve each other." she turned and started to walk away.

"By the way, you aren't that good. She is faking it."

Rebecca tried moving past Kevin. Kevin rushed towards her before she could walk through the door, "Don't you ever come here unannounced again? Do you understand me? You have no right to talk to her that way."

"I have every damn right. She ruined my marriage."

"No sweetheart, our marriage was ruined before she came into the picture."

"Fuck you Kevin!" she said as Kevin pushed her out of his office.

Chapter 45

Cheryl reached her car and fell to pieces. Her cell phone began to ring.

"Babe, where are you. I have been at your place for almost an hour," Matthew said.

"I-I...can we do this some other night?"

"What's wrong?"

"Nothing, I'm just....." Cheryl started crying uncontrollably. "It was his secretary all along. He has been screwing her under my nose all this time."

"Babe, where are you? Come home and we can talk...." Matthew said into the receiver.

Cheryl hung up the phone. She drove until she came to the first liquor store she could find. She needed something to calm her nerves. She drank half of the Bacardi before getting home. She could feel the buzz take over.

She staggered into the house and flung herself onto the sofa. Matthew came over to check on her.

"Babe, it's ok," he said while kneeling in front of her.

Cheryl looked up as she felt his hand on her leg. The alcohol was really altering her decision-making process. She reached up and pulled his head close to hers then kissed him passionately. She pushed her tongue into his mouth, kissed his ears, and his neck. His hands wrapped around her waist. She needed to put Kevin out of her mind.

"Do you want me?" She asked him between kisses.

"Yes, but..." she covered his mouth again with hers. She pushed him back onto the couch and straddled him.

"Take me Matthew," she urged him.

"But..." she put her finger to his mouth, letting him know with a look that it was what she wanted too.

Matthew pulled her sweater over her head, and hungrily eyed her breasts. His hands nimbly unfastened her bra then pulled the straps down and took one plump breast in his mouth. Her breath came quick and choppy. She threw her head back as she held his head to her.

"Oh God," she heard him moan.

His primal instincts took over. He needed to be inside of her. In one quick motion he rolled her over and stripped away his clothes while he pulled her legs free from her jeans. She hadn't yet released her other leg before he was back on top of her, his erection pressing between her thighs.

She moved her legs, squeezing his manhood while working herself into a frenzy. "Ohhhh!" She cried out as a wave of pleasure washed over her. He moaned and threw her legs back, plunging himself deep into her.

"Give it to me," she cried out.

"You like this don't you?" Matthew asked breathlessly. She could only nod in agreement as another orgasm swept through her.

"That's right baby. Give it to me."

Cheryl tried to find something to hold onto because he was rocking her world. She grabbed his arms, and his moans grew louder.

"Open your eyes Cheryl," he moaned. "I want you to see me when I cum inside of you."

His body tightened against hers, his eyes bore straight into her soul, his mouth came crashing down on hers, hungrily searching for her tongue. The passion in that kiss was incredible. He pushed himself into her for another minute before finally collapsing on top of her.

She maneuvered herself from under him, and found a tear rolling down her face. Cheryl thought back to one moment in her marriage when she knew Kevin wasn't her knight in shining armor on a white horse, but the devil riding in on the black one.

They had just finished having sex for the third time that night and Kevin was still wanting more. She couldn't take anymore and by the time he came again, she was pushing him off of her. They hadn't been intimate since the honeymoon because she had gotten a bladder infection, so at least she had a two week reprieve. But since the doctor had cleared her earlier that day, it was like he was a dog in heat.

"What the hell is your problem?"

"Kevin, my God. I'm sore. Do you not see that I am not in the mood anymore, gosh."

"Lookahere, you are my wife and whenever I feel like having sex with you, I will, so I suggest you get some baby oil or something, because if you knew what the fuck you were doing, I could get off without having to screw you half the night. I see why nobody wanted to be bothered with your ass, you acted like your shit is all that and it's not!"

Matthew was still asleep when she came downstairs with her suitcase. She looked down on him and picked up her keys, left the note and walked out the door. Did he really enjoy this, or was Kevin right?

Cheryl never felt that she deserved anyone that treated her well. She wasn't the prettiest girl, or the girl that boys wanted to be around. She was the ugly duckling, hoping that someone would pay some attention to her and when Shaun turned out to be the first one, she thought she would be with him forever.

That didn't happen and from that point she didn't know if her standards were too high or if the standards of the men she wanted to date were. Realistically she should be happy with whomever she dated, because like her mother always told her, she was the smart one and she should be glad that any boy wanted her.

Chapter 46

Matthew woke up by himself and it gave him a chance to think of all that happened. He was finally able to make love to her, slow and easy and he couldn't believe he had developed feelings for this woman. The way she ran her fingers over his back made him smile and the way she whispered and moaned his name just before she climaxed had him wanting more of her. His mind was clouded with thoughts of how he wished his mom were here to meet this woman.

Cheryl was the woman he could spend the rest of his life with. He wanted forever with this woman. She was sexy, smart and most of all she loved her kids. This was the kind of woman he wanted, no; this was the kind of woman he needed in his life and he would make sure she knew it.

He got up and decided to find her because his body told him that he wanted more of what he had last night. His heart told him that he didn't want to be without her. He went upstairs, hoping she was in the shower. He didn't find her. He ran back downstairs, pulled on his pants and as he was about to leave the den, he saw the purple paper.

I need to take some time away. Last night was wonderful. You made me feel like a woman again. I don't know all of the emotions I am feeling right now but I hope you understand that I need to think about all that has happened.

Cheryl

He let the paper fall from his hand and his mind began to race. He wasn't going to let her get away that easy. He wanted to be with her so much that he could barely drive himself home. He wasn't ready to let go of the afterglow of last night and he would move mountains to make sure that he was able to keep that feeling.

- To be continued -

COMING IN 2015

Check out this Excerpt from

Let Me Just Say This...Again

Chapter 1

Matthew woke up by himself. He found his pants and pulled them up his muscular legs, then set about the house to find her. He searched, but all signs pointed to the fact that she was not there.

He pulled his sweater on and as he headed out the front door he found the note. He read it over and over, hoping that it was some kind of mistake but she was gone. Just like that, she left without a word, unless you count the note to him. He crumpled the paper in his hand and went to his car, letting the door slam.

He got home and needed to figure out how he was going to find her. She said she needed time to think, time to sort things out. She always spoke about going to Florida whenever she felt stressed and hoping this is hunch was right, he called her mother.

Spending fifteen minutes on the phone with her didn't help his mood but he was able to get some clues as to where she might be. He showered, shaved and packed an overnight bag. He needed to travel light just in case he was wrong.

He arrived at the airport hoping to find a seat on the first thing out of D.C. to Florida. He hoped his luck in finding a seat on the next plane was going to continue but seeing the crowd of passengers who had gotten bumped, his prospect didn't look good.

"Good afternoon, I am hoping that you can help me," he said as he walked up to the counter, "I am trying to get a first class seat to Florida."

"Oh, sir, I'm sorry. All of our flights to Florida are totally booked. Matter of fact, we have some passengers on stand-by trying to get there. With this weather being what it is, everybody wants to get out of town."

Not to be discouraged he continued as if she hadn't said a word.

"Well, it's a matter of life and death. I really need to get to Florida as soon as possible. Is there any way you can find me a flight?"

He smiled and leaned against the counter, "I would appreciate it."

"Let me check for you."

She started tapping keys and looking at the screen. "I'm sorry, sir, there is nothing. Even if it were, I would be obligated to get these other passengers on first, since they have been waiting for over two hours."

"Please, can you look again?" Matthew was not above begging.

Again she went back to tapping the keys. She spoke just above a whisper. "Well there is a flight that has a seat, in first class, but it is going to run you at least nine hundred and fifty-two dollars, and that's before all of the fees."

"I'll take it!" he handed her his black American Express card.

"The flight is leaving from Gate 12 in twenty minutes. Do you have any bags that you need checked?"

"No."

She printed out the boarding pass and handed it to him.

"Thank you very much, Linda. You just made me

the happiest man in the world. I will never forget this."

"No problem. Enjoy yourself Mr. Perry," she said with a smile.

Matthew called the flower shop within the airport and had them make a special arrangement for Linda, just to show his appreciation. After taking his seat, he quickly took out his laptop, and logged into his AOL account. He shot off a quick note to Terry, told him what was going on and for him to call the Sheraton in Miami to book a room. Matthew sat back, closed his eyes and thought just how lucky he had been.

Cheryl woke up feeling refreshed but tired at the same time. Her flight landed late and she was too wired to go to sleep. She sat up all night thinking of Matthew and how she should have told him where she was going.

Her phone rang, breaking her trance.

"Where the fuck are you?" came the irate voice from the other end.

"None of your business."

"It's my fucking business when you up and leave Kayla with your parents and don't tell them where the fuck you are going."

"Kevin, look, whatever I do or don't do, is none of your business."

"Don't get cute with me, Cheryl. I am not going to have you running off whenever the mood strikes you."

"What do you care, what kind of mood I'm in?"

"Bitch!" Kevin yelled.

She pressed the end button and set the phone down. It began to ring again. She picked it up expecting to hear Kevin cursing.

"Hey sexy. Don't think you are going to get away from me that easily. I'll see you soon."

She didn't get to say anything because the caller

hung up. It wasn't a voice she recognized. She went to the bathroom and decided to soak in some bubbles for a little while before starting her day.

LOOK FOR MORE IN 2015!

B. Swangin Webster

Biography

B. Swangin Webster continues to birth her characters and is continuously amazed at how "life-like" they become. They all vie for her attention and will "talk" to her at the most inopportune times.

In 2008, after encouragement from her oldest daughter, B. Swangin Webster dived in head first into the deep end of the publishing world. Although she wasn't a graceful swimmer, she quickly adapted, when Publish America threw her a life jacket and told her to swim over to their company. Her debut novel; Let Me Just Say This was published less than three weeks after submission in November of 2008.

While basking in the glow of having her first novel published, she quickly realized that being an author was something that she had always dreamed of. She also realized that the sequel to Let Me Just Say This, was already written. She had to trim down her debut novel and what was left over, is now the novel; And Again...Let Me Say This. This novel was released in October 2009, less than a year after her debut novel hit the book stores.

CPSIA information can be obtained at www.ICGtesting.com
Printed in the USA
LVOW10s1838150914

404140LV00008B/1030/P